W9-CCH-585

UNIVERSITY OF CALGARY
Press

DISAPPEARING IN REVERSE

a novel(la)

PAPL
DISCARDED

Allie McFarland

Brave & Brilliant Series
ISSN 2371-7238 (Print) ISSN 2371-7246 (Online)

© 2020 Allie McFarland

University of Calgary Press
2500 University Drive NW
Calgary, Alberta
Canada T2N 1N4
press.ucalgary.ca

This book is available as an ebook. The publisher should be contacted for any use which falls outside the terms of that license.

This is a work of fiction. Names, characters, businesses, places, events and incidents are either the products of the author's imagination or used in a fictitious manner. Any resemblance to actual persons, living or dead, or actual events is purely coincidental.

LIBRARY AND ARCHIVES CANADA CATALOGUING IN PUBLICATION

Title: Disappearing in reverse : a novel(la) / Allie McFarland.
Names: McFarland, Allie, 1993- author.
Series: Brave & brilliant series ; no. 16.
Description: Series statement: Brave & brilliant series, 2371-7238 ; no. 16
Identifiers: Canadiana (print) 20200182641 | Canadiana (ebook) 2020018265X
 | ISBN 9781773851433 (softcover) | ISBN 9781773851440 (PDF) | ISBN
 9781773851457 (EPUB) | ISBN 9781773851464 (Kindle)
Classification: LCC PS8625.F375 D57 2020 | DDC C813/.6—dc23

The University of Calgary Press acknowledges the support of the Government of Alberta through the Alberta Media Fund for our publications. We acknowledge the financial support of the Government of Canada. We acknowledge the financial support of the Canada Council for the Arts for our publishing program.

Printed and bound in Canada by Marquis
♻ This book is printed on Enviro Book Antique paper

Editing by Naomi K. Lewis
Cover image: Colourbox 28717842 and 36554209
Cover design, page design, and typesetting by Melina Cusano

DISAPPEARING IN REVERSE

For Lissa McFarland

The back of my company van is occupied by an empty gurney with rumpled sheets. Mr. Frank Johnston, who was wrapped under them, sits in the passenger seat, belted upright, my spare sunglasses over his sinking eyes. Drumming on the steering wheel to the radio, I detour into a McDonalds drive-thru. Frank won't sing with me, which is fair—him being dead and all.

After months of rain, the sun finally made an appearance through wispy clouds, and though it's only March and twelve degrees, it sure feels like winter's over. The radio blasts a summer hit from a few years back, and I sing along, trying not to think of Devin. Today's a good day—sunshine, and I'm alive. I set my bar low to maximize good days, but with the amount of cloud cover in Victoria, turns out it's not so low.

"Hi there, what can I get for you?" A voice warbles through the speaker.

"I'll have a swirl cone."

"Anything else?"

Glance at Frank, immobile. "No, that's all."

"Fifty-six cents."

I pull forward, hand a loonie to the boy who passes the ice cream, a quarter, and other change through the window.

The boy glances at my passenger, the van logo: *Mourning Glory*. His lips part, but I don't give him time to ask. I toss the coins into my cup holder for my next ice-cream run and merge into traffic licking my cone. Not that there's much traffic in the middle of the day. I avoid spilling cream over my fingers or onto the seat. It's a bit tasteless—Dairy Queen is better, but they don't have drive-thrus. And the recently deceased deserve one last hoorah.

The route to the funeral home should take fifteen minutes. Instead, I weave through residential streets and playground zones, and make a brief stop in a school parking lot when my ice cream's finished. I unbuckle Mr. Frank Johnston, sling his arm over my shoulder like he's had a few too many drinks and I'm helping him stumble into a taxi, and heave him onto the gurney. Take my sunglasses back once he's all tucked in for the ride. Good thing he's old and small, mostly just a bag of skin for rattling bones.

Every detail in order, we proceed the next few blocks at a solemn pace until I slide into the stall in the back reserved for deliveries.

"Kramer!" I call out the open window.

"Hey! What've you got for me today?"

"A retired real estate mogul from Oak Bay. Pancreatic cancer finally got him." Kramer knows this. He sent me on the pickup.

"Poor bugger. His wife'll make sure there's lots of flowers."

"Tulips and daffodils. She didn't seem like a rosy person." I hop out of the van, "Second wife, at least twenty years younger."

We light cigarettes, leaning against the vehicle.

Kramer inhales, "Well," blows smoke out his nose, "at least she has time to find another husband."

I close my eyes and feel the sun on my face, slight breeze, the sharp tang of cigarette smoke in my mouth. Frank won't mind waiting a little longer for his box.

At seven p.m. I'm sitting in my self-regulation class. Actually, I should be in class, but I'm jogging across the grass, two coffees in hand, five minutes late. When I told Dad about the course, he joked that it sounded like something from the hospital—not wrong. I think one of the group sessions may have had the same name. But this is a political science class and all about how "the government implements and promotes good social behaviour through reward / punishment programs and surveillance" and whatever else. They say this helps "enforce self-regulatory behaviour in the general population." I'm not convinced it isn't another form of social control that leads to blind obedience. Rae and I whisper about the bullshit and how governments obviously want docile citizens— she from her Lekwungen roots, and I from a general sense of resistance and rebellion. The prof sees her points, but disagrees with mine, as per his comments on my last paper. "Juvenile and underdeveloped." I rolled my eyes when I read that feedback and promptly recycled my fifteen-page essay.

Anyway, Rae's acing the class, and she saves me a seat in the second-to-back row, so I bring her a vanilla latte. I get the same because it's easy to order. "A vanilla latte, medium. Actually, make that two," or "two medium vanilla lattes, please." Such a nice-sounding order, but the syrup coats my teeth so they feel furry, fuzzy, and I can't understand why Rae likes this drink so much. One day she joked that *it's an attempt to blend in with basic white girls*, but I think she genuinely enjoys the flavour. Somewhere between too sweet and too bitter. I always want to order a tea for myself, but can't decide what type. Do I want chamomile? Earl Grey? Cream of Earl Grey? What's the difference between those? What's a rooibos? And do I want a tea latte or just steeped tea? Faced with a barista and an intimidating line of tea bags, I panic, and resort to copying Rae's order. She emails me all the class notes the day before exams, as my notes have large gaps where I doze

3

off. I bring the coffee, and I'm always late, mostly to prove that the prof's measures for *self-regulation* don't work on me.

APARTMENT

When I get home, I fill a pot with water, set to boil, and measure a cup of rice. Then open the fridge and pull out the bundle of bok choy. After chopping a few stalks and throwing them in a pan with grapeseed oil, I meander to my room and change into pyjamas. Once the rice is ready, I mix in the bok choy and a spoonful of butter. No roommate means I can leave the knife on the counter for a few days. I take the pot and a fork to the coffee table and scroll through Facebook on my phone as I eat. Not that there's anything interesting. A few status updates about so-and-so enjoying too many drinks, someone really liking tacos, and a few people claiming homework makes their face twitch or causes compulsive swearing. All people from high school or forced group projects in elective classes that aren't really electives because you need take them or else you can't graduate. I don't really pay attention to who posts what. The same internet pictures and memes circulate every few months. And then.

A photograph, black and white, stares at me from the screen. Not that the girl herself is staring. Straight hair covers the right side of her face, the other side turned profile. Her nose. Her nose is what I recognize. An irregular bump on the bridge, the tip upturned. She broke it almost six years ago. Rather, I broke it.

I fill two plastic pitchers with ice and water and pick the bathroom lock with a penny. It's a flat line, easy to twist. We're in the middle of a prank war. Devin's showering, but we've seen each other naked before, and I yank the curtain back to douse her. Arms up, fingers lathering soap in her hair. My attack hits her from the neck down. I run. I manage to refill my pitchers and dash outside before Devin thunders downstairs. Panting, I hide underneath the back deck. It's raised, so I can stand and crane my neck up, see through the cracks between the wood panels, be ready when she comes out. Before she realizes I'm down here, I jump onto the stairs, swinging my water pitchers. Too exuberant. One jug empties over her still soapy head, the other connects with her nose. Blood doesn't gush yet, but drip, drip, drips. Over her top lip, onto her white front teeth. Two breaths, that's all I wait. I start running before Devin, but she's faster than me. And smarter. She grabs the hose and drenches me, unconcerned about her own soaked and unravelled robe. We collapse into a wet heap, laughing.

That's how I remember it. Us laughing, drenched, and hugging. No need for forgiveness because neither of us was harmed. But she was hurt. Her nose, broken, gushed blood so bright red in the sun, even as she twisted the knob to turn on the hose. Devin's pain obvious, she dropped the hose and curled into herself, into the puddle forming on the ground, and I ran to her. I will always run to her. And I coiled around her, hid my tears and my shame in the cold water, but she noticed anyway. "What the hell are you crying for? You're the one who broke my damn nose!" She picked up the hose and doused my face so I could barely breathe, and we both sat up. Soaking and muddy and bloody.

And then we laughed.

In my memory, I like to skip the pain and the crying. Go straight to the laughter. How her eyes pinch to slits when she smiles.

That was the day we both got hypothermia in the middle of summer. The summer she came to live with me. 2008. One year before she died. But now her image stares at me with the caption: *she is not dead.*

I shut my computer and go to bed, leaving the full pot on the table.

The next morning, I open Facebook on my phone, and the photo makes eye contact with me again. Devin's shoulder angled up to avoid questions, her collarbone highlighted by the shadow underneath. I don't recognize the source. Maybe it's shared by a friend of a friend? Doesn't matter—I save the image. Go to work.

No pickups today, so I'm with Kramer, fixing a woman's makeup while he attends the casket and viewing room. Usually he deals with making the bodies presentable, but he thinks I have a knack and doesn't trust the florist to arrange the bouquets with "the correct air of propriety," whatever that means. All I know is dead people don't flinch, and doing them up doesn't take long. Except the hair. It has to sit in rollers with extra-strength hairspray until an hour before viewing. Not that the hair itself is too different on people living and dead, but it can break off because of the embalming, so I—gently—comb the strands into place when the rollers come out. Everyone who dies gets curled hair; straight hair makes them look too dead.

Aesthetics rely on light touches.

Other than the hair, I always finish with the lipstick because the glue between the lips needs to dry. I start with blush. Gawking mourners prefer their lost ones to look like they were, rather than as they are. A healthy glow to imagine a loved one, lover, sleeping. Breaths so shallow their chest doesn't quiver, face forever on the verge of revealing a smile. Small discs under the eyelids for the impression of eyes. Not that Kramer removes the real eyes—those stay with the rest of the body, but they sink into the skull, floating downward into their sockets just like how the rest of the body lowers into the ground.

Sometimes I talk to my clients about this farce. They humour me by staying silent. No reason to care about my sponge on their cheeks, brush smudging sparkles at the corners of their eyes. Not now. At least they don't have to worry about pimples from unclean makeup brushes. But I don't talk to this woman, because she's lying on her back in a polyester suit provided by her husband. She has no time for small talk. Or large talk. Just plain business. Maybe I think of her that way because I know she died of an aneurism. And spent the last forty-three years as a hotel manager. It's a pity she wore out before her shoulder padded suit—in two months she'll be a skeleton and still dressed for work.

Finished with her touch-ups, Kramer and I break for lunch. We don't eat during our breaks, instead, we stand outside the back door, in the driveway with our pickup van, smoking. Under an overhang, the drizzle doesn't touch us.

I pull out my phone and show him Devin's picture. "Ever seen this?"

"No, should I have?"

"Do you recognize her?"

He flicks the ash from his cigarette, "Not really."

"But sort of?"

"Looks a bit like Cameron Wittaker, the gymnast from two winters back."

Cameron Wittaker, a lean girl, all limbs, who ended on Kramer's slab after a trick on the vault went wrong. Her arms stretched over the beam, head hit it straight on, bending her chin into her throat. Instantaneous. "Poor girl," everyone said, "She was going somewhere." Cameron Wittaker was my first pick up, the January roads terrible because of the snow. Her whole family waited for me, tear stained and crumpled like tissues matted with snot. And I thought the weather was grieving, too.

But she wasn't Devin.

"I think she looks like Devin. Devin Evans." I tuck my phone in my back pocket.

"Devin?" Kramer remembers most faces he's buried. He keeps photographs of them before the makeup is done. He remembers the skin bare, stripped down. But he wouldn't have done Devin's makeup—she was cremated. "No, not a thing like Devin. Her hair was more red. Not so dark."

If he can remember a distinction of shade, he must have taken her photo just before turning her to ash. "You can't tell that from a black-and-white picture." I toss my butt and slam through the door, even though our break's not over.

I stop by my dad's, where Devin lived with me. He's sure to have any old photos, just so I can be certain the girl in the picture isn't Devin. Kramer won't let me see his photos—he claims not to have them. My dad keeps a key inside the plastic flowerpot beside the front door. Holding the door open with my foot, I replace the key and step inside. I remove my shoes on the mat, leave them haphazard. Old habits.

"Dad!" Maybe I should've knocked first, but he doesn't answer. Neither does Bethany, his girlfriend.

Probably out running Saturday errands, like usual. Stocking up on dishwasher detergent and groceries. Or maybe he's over at her place in Sidney. Doesn't matter, I can find what I need.

I head for the basement first. We never kept photo albums, but I'm sure there's a box of stuff from my old room with some pictures. Devin and me laughing about the next grand scheme we'd planned or just pulled off. Stealing all the flowers planted along the main road's median in the middle of the night. Or wrapping glitter in long sheets of clingwrap and taping them to the front windows of the local Fairways grocery store. It's almost impossible to take down the glitter sheets without exploding it over yourself. This was before phone cameras were any good—and we would take photos on our shared digital camera, print them all on glossy paper, pin them to our walls with thumbtacks and tape, and delete the originals. Something romantic about the idea of impermanence.

IN REVERSE

Midnight holds a certain fascination for us. The front door too risky, we shimmy through the basement window. Flick spiders out of our faces as they attempt to weave across our threshold. We could sneak out any time the sky got dark enough, any time after ten, but midnight's the only time we venture out. Maybe because it's the turning of the day, welcoming the morning before its arrival. More likely because our stories sound cooler when they happened at midnight. And we always fabricate our stories.

I find the boxes labelled *My Crap* in thick marker stacked under the window we used to crawl through, crammed between a shelf of empty mason jars and a ratty ironing board. I lift the first one down and sit cross-legged. Inside are old stuffed animals. A ballcap wearing owl my mom gave me when I joined softball, a unicorn whose horn glows when squeezed. A pair of black dance shoes, the elastic strap torn off one, the toe duct taped to the sole on the other, both balls worn smooth. No pictures. The next box holds a sheep-shaped piggy bank, class yearbooks from high school, and clothes I didn't want but couldn't part with. Jeans with holes strategically crafted by a butter knife and tweezers in the knees, thighs, back pockets. My "Wednesday hoodie," a lime green abomination with stains on the cuffs and a broken zipper. In the third box I find some pictures, but none of Devin.

Pictures I took of myself blowing kisses to the camera. Tits half dangling out of a too-small bra, harsh red lipstick. A mini skirt that looks more like a cropped tube top. I took those pictures before I got into trouble, when I was only practising in the bathroom mirror. The bathtub and fish-patterned shower curtain in the background. When I was fourteen and on top of the world. Before I knew Devin.

Then photobooth strips, six of us squished too close. Evidence of someone's hand on someone's crotch and my tongue in someone else's mouth. Eyes identically large and cracked with red veins. We would go to the mall after school or instead of school. Couldn't afford anything, but came home with handfuls of makeup, nail polish, black tights. We were misunderstood. I was young—easily influenced, led astray.

More pictures, from after my brief stint at the ward. Me and my dad sporting matching sweaters and smiles in front of a Christmas tree. My hands on the ferry railing, hair falling over my face, swirling in the wind and salt spray, back when my hair was dyed black and hung to my waist. No Devin.

Above me a jangle, then a few muffled thumps. The door must've run over my shoes.

"Hello? Hi?"

My concentration broken, I look up from my abandoned stuff, things from a past life, so far away and still so close. My response comes a few beats later than normal, and my voice cracks a bit as I call, "Down here, Dad."

Clomp, clomp, clomp.

"What on earth are you doing?" He shakes his head, and I realize how I must look, sitting cross-legged in the midst of boxes.

"Looking for pictures of Devin."

He shakes his head. "They won't be in your boxes, sweetheart. I think I saved a few from your purge, in my filing cabinet."

Sitting in my room, thumb tacks scattered on the floor, walls left almost empty. Every picture of Devin in my hands. The two of us hugging a red wrong-way sign in Paris. The two of us bruised and paint splattered after paintball. The two of us making duck faces at the camera, on the beach, the ocean behind us, winking. Us two, in every picture. Together. Sprawled on towels at Durrance Lake, with matching bikinis, our white skin sunburnt in the same place on our shoulders. Flushed faces smushed side by side, with bright pink lipstick. One by one, I tear the images into confetti squares. The corner of someone's eye, linked fingers, pieces of blue and orange skies. How could she leave me?

I toss everything back into the boxes and follow my dad upstairs.

"Here. Are you looking for a specific picture?" He opens the drawer third from the top and extracts a folder labelled *Europe, 2009.* Our last family trip, five years ago now. Not that we went on any before that.

"No."

"You won't wreck these, right? You're done blaming yourself?" He passes me the folder, and continues before I answer. "Do you want lunch or anything?"

We head to the kitchen, and I don't see any evidence of grocery shopping. No plastic bags on the counter. Maybe he was at the bank, doing other adult stuff.

"Grilled cheese?" I fiddle with the manila case, bend the tab at the top so I can't see the date. I don't need the reminder of how long it's been. Or hasn't been.

"And iced tea?" Nothing in his house ever changes.

"Sounds good to me." I smile, and sit at the raised table. Spread the folder's contents in front of me.

A map of the London underground and ticket stubs. We jumped the turnstiles the day we bought the wrong tickets and couldn't get through. A hotel pen from Copthorne. Odd-shaped change in a plastic sandwich bag. And a stack of photos, the ones Dad had developed at Wal-Mart, held together with two elastic bands, one thick and blue, the other thin and beige. All the memories I didn't want to keep.

A pan rattles on the stove, butter sizzles.

I flip through the images, old buildings and statues flashing passed. Strangers walking, holding hands, gesturing, pointing cameras aimlessly. Hidden in the middle are five photos of the three of us—Devin, Dad, and me—that he'd asked random people to take. In front of Buckingham Palace, on the Pont des Arts Bridge, and other, less identifiable places, all posed, stiff. They don't tell a story. Dad kept them. Chose these images to save from my "purge." I line them up—we're so small next to the grandeur of culture and history, it's hard to make out individual details. The bump on Devin's nose.

Opening my phone, I compare it to the relics of our trip.

"Here," Dad says, setting a plate and glass in front of me.

I glance at the golden sandwich, Kraft Singles cheese oozing orange from the diagonal slice. "Thanks."

"Why the sudden interest?" He sits beside me with his own sandwich.

I hold up my phone with Devin's picture.

"Who is this?"

"Devin. She has the same nose."

"So do you, so do lots of people." He bites off almost a quarter of his grilled cheese in one go. Chews slow.

"But it has to be her. As soon as I saw it, I knew."

He looks at me, puts his grilled cheese back on his plate, and extends his greasy hand over mine.

"Dad."

He withdraws his comfort. "She died, sweetie, and it sucks, but it was no one's fault."

He's wrong. We both know it was all my fault. I take a bite of my sandwich—the melted cheese refuses to separate from the main and dangles between my mouth and the bread.

"No one could have known she'd get sick. That her body couldn't take it." Dad bites his knuckle and looks out the window, away from me. "But we have photos and our memories to keep her alive. Inside us."

My sandwich feels suddenly cold. I drop it.

Dad clears our still-full plates off the table. "Please, don't ruin these pictures."

"You did this! My baby's dead because of you!" Slams my shoulders against my dad's kitchen wall.

Aunt Jocelyn's nails in my skin. Her hair falling from its bun.

"I didn't do anything!" Devin, where are you? Tell your mom it isn't my fault!

Eyes smeared with makeup, puffy, red veined. Flecks of saliva fly from her teeth, hit my nose, cheeks.

"Streptococcus. It comes from strep throat. You're the reason my daughter got sick! The reason she died!"

Her hands quiver. Release. Devin's mom falls. Knees collapse, her fists on the hardwood floor. Sobbing, howling. I'm glued to the wall, stuck. Watch Dacy enter, hold her mom.

Twelve years old, small for her age, smoothing her mom's hair because her sister died.

"It'll be okay, Mom, it'll be okay." Dacy kneels, rocks with her, hugging and murmuring. Not even looking at me. "We're going to be okay."

I'm the one saving a seat for Rae next self-regulation class, both our coffees perched on the empty desk beside me. Waiting, waiting, I tap my pen, bounce my foot against the floor, tip back on my chair legs and let them swing down, thudding in place. Repeat. Ten minutes before class begins, she arrives, bag slung over her shoulder and textbooks in her arms.

"Hi, you're early." Rae falls into her desk.

"It's been known to happen." I can't stop fidgeting, curling the corners of my notebook pages.

Rae raises her eyebrows at my fingers but just teases, "Since when?"

"About fifteen minutes ago, when I sat down." I make an effort to smile at her.

She just shakes her head and takes her coffee.

I switch back to tapping my pen, lid down, on Devin's picture. The regular pressure ensuring the screen doesn't go dark.

"Is that the she's-not-dead girl?" Rae turns my phone towards her, interrupting my rhythm.

"Yeah, do you recognize her?" I chew on my pen lid.

Rae grabs her coffee and takes a swig. "Only from the internet ad."

"Ad? No, it's from Facebook."

"Yeah, Facebook has ads." She squints her eyes at me, confused.

"On the side, not in the main feed."

"Where have you been? They've been running ads in the main feed for like a year now!"

I look back at my phone, the photo, Devin's photo, screen captured. And yes, below, it does say "sponsored ad," but what for? No company name on the image I saved.

"Anyway," Rae continues, "I'm pretty sure it's an AIDS awareness campaign or something. You know, a *this terrible disease doesn't kill right away—get educated you morons* type of ad they're always running."

My mouth, dry, I squeak out, "Who is?"

"I don't know. The government? Social service people?" She drinks more of her coffee and shrugs. "It's the type of shit this class is teaching us about. Shaming citizens into compliance and blah blah blah."

I put my pen down and reach into my bag for the picture I got from my dad.

"Doesn't it look like her?"

Rae points to me, "Her? Sure, I guess."

"No, the other girl."

"A bit. But she's so small in the frame, you can't really tell. The internet picture barely shows her face." Sips more of her latte. "Anyway, you know I can't tell you white people apart." Rae laughs, probably trying to lighten my mood.

Doesn't work. I put my phone and the picture into my bag and stand. "Mind sending me today's notes? I'm not feeling well."

"You know finals are in two weeks, right?" She raises both eyebrows at me this time, two perfectly symmetrically plucked arches.

I don't bother responding. Abandon my latte on the desk, take my bag and leave, sliding past the professor in the doorway. He rolls his eyes at me, doesn't understand my leaving has nothing to do with our mutual animosity, nothing to do with him.

APARTMENT

At home, I take a hot shower. Let the water pound me until I'm crouched in the bathtub, running my fingers over the swirling pattern on my anti-slip mat. I try to breathe but can only gasp inwards. No air escapes. My stomach pulses in, out, in, out, my bellybutton disappearing and reappearing in a fold of skin and pudge. I can't take any more air. I rock on my heels, mouth open, water hissing over my cheeks and down my chin. No sound except for the water. And it sounds like the blood drip, drip, dripping from Devin's nose over her teeth stained pink. But faster, faster. Dripping in my hair, down my back, my arms, legs. Not my teeth, my white teeth. Molars clattering as the water gets colder. My shoulders clench against the downpour.

Eyes closed, I unwrap myself and reach for the tap, turn off the water. Curl back into my limbs and imagine curling around Devin, the soft mud beneath us.

The feeling, the feeling I've only had twice before.

Once, when I was starting junior high and my dad told me about my mom. My real mom. That she died when I was born. But the mom I lived with, how she chose me, and she loved me.

Of jumping on a mattress. Lurching, stumbling, unstable footing.

And sitting at home, on the couch without Devin. They said she died. They told me at school, and then I don't know how I got home to the couch that seems empty even though all my family's here. All except Devin, except the one who matters. They tell me and they tell me and then they sit in silence. No one repeats the words. Perhaps it just echoes in my mind. They couldn't save her. They couldn't save her.

That feeling, now, seeing Devin's photo. And then stepping onto solid ground and crashing in a flurry of knees, elbows, fists. But only in my head.

I'm still in bed at eleven, rain drizzling at my window. So much for getting to my ten o'clock class. Face in my pillow, blankets over my head. Two hours later, I take my fluffy blanket with me to the kitchen and put on the kettle for tea. I try to do the reading for my Renegade Women English class, but van Herk's novel can't hold my attention. *No Fixed Address*, an old book that Devin loved, after she found it buried in a box in Dad's basement. She read it on a similarly drizzly afternoon, all in one go, closed it decisively.

"But where did she actually go, physically? There's no way she just vanished into the Great White North. There aren't enough men up there for her." Devin bit the inside of her lip, like she was really thinking through the ratio of men to landscape. "No, if you want to hide—if I were going to hide—a big city is the way to go. Just meld in with everyone else. Anonymous."

I hadn't read the book, and I didn't have a response.

Dad walked through the living room and picked up the novel from the coffee table. "Please don't go through my old boxes." He walked away, still carrying the book, "This is Millie's." His first wife's. My birth mother's. Sometimes I think she's gone, but her things linger, contained in unlabelled boxes.

I didn't read it, couldn't find the book or that box again. I forgot about it, until I needed an English credit to graduate, and I saw Aritha van Herk's book on the course list. The copy I have now is new-to-me, from the consignment bookstore on campus. A blue cover with smeared leaves, like a photo taken from a car window. I think the copy Devin read—the one that was my birth mom's and then my dad's—was pink with a grey road down the middle. The bookstore only had the one cover design, and I picked a copy plastered with *used* stickers and decorated with highlighter marks inside. The worse the condition, the cheaper the book. Could have saved money and asked Dad for his copy, but I don't think he'd appreciate if I marked up those pages with my own scribbles and highlighted sentences.

The main character is a travelling underwear saleswoman, Arachne, who sleeps around with lots of men while she has the perfect boyfriend at home in Calgary. As far as I can tell, the writer wasn't concerned with creating a normal story plot. Arachne drives an old Mercedes, tries to ignore her rough childhood, gets involved with a really old guy, and tells all her stories to her best friend, and finally vanishes. I'm only a little ways in, at the part in the cemetery with an old man and an exposed skull, but the prof doesn't care about spoilers, so I sort of know where she's going. Eventually, Arachne will go north, unless Devin lied to me about that part.

I'm having trouble reading the story—dreading having to write an essay about the structure or the narrator, dreading talking about the characters in a class with fifty other tired students. If I could talk to Devin about the book, then maybe I'd want to finish it.

Tossing *No Fixed Address* aside, I look around my living room. My pot with rice and bok choy borders on mouldering on the table. Stray socks litter the floor, the crevasses between couch cushions. Dust coats the TV stand. The bag from the Shoppers I stopped at last night lies beside the door, where I dropped it when I came in. I stand and retrieve the bottle of black hair dye, and leave the plastic bag beside my shoes. Clean out the sink, find an old towel, remove my shirt, and put on the disposable gloves from the package. With my hair flipped over my face I apply the dye, squirting blindly and rubbing. I tie my hair in a high bun, the kind I had to wear when I danced as a kid, but not nearly as neat. Thirty minutes pass without me noticing the time, but the alarm on my phone buzzes to tell me. Rinse.

I forgot to make my tea, so I flip the kettle's switch again and wrap myself in my blanket without putting my shirt on. Catch myself in the bathroom mirror. Dark, my hair, like when I went through my emo phase. Like when Devin first came to live with me.

No use. I leave the kettle boiling, throw on a sweater and yoga pants. It's still raining, no need to dry my hair. Grab my keys, wallet, cigarettes, and flip flops. In my car I don't pause, don't drum my palms on the wheel, just shift into drive and go. I think I'll head to the marina, but instead I turn away from the core and hit the highway. Smaller than the work van, my car weaves through other cars that insist on the speed limit. Twenty minutes later, I'm forced to slow down through Broadmead with its big houses that pay me no mind. Down Cordova Bay Road, where the trees reach for each other. Slow to thirty kilometres an hour though the posted limit is forty so I don't miss the turn off for Agate Lane, hidden between the trees. Find the empty parking lot and stop in a puddle. No one comes to this beach, it's all rocks and bird shit and dead trees. The rain comes harder now.

AGATE LANE BEACH

I walk through the small grassy area with shaded picnic tables, into the open sand. Arms spread to the ocean, rain tangling through my hair, over my shoulders. This is what I was searching for. I abandon my shoes and walk to the ocean's edge, raising small pools of water in the indents left by my heels, toes. Cold. I place my hands in the water where ocean and sand knit. Together. Knead the silt with my fingers, finding stones and shells. Close my eyes. My fingers move slower, slower, so I feel every pull against the ridges of my fingerprints. Not prints yet. The water can't discern where I touch. My fingerprints don't exist here.

Back in my car, covered in salt and melted raindrops, I light a cigarette with the window open. The smoke blurs with the haze over the ocean.

IN REVERSE

Devin tells me she wants to escape. Her hand cupped to my ear like we're children. And maybe we are. Or maybe that's just the effect the hospital has on everyone. Her breath warming my neck, she says she'll get out of here, one way or another. Tells me that's why she's been keen on exploring the different wards and back stairways. Tells me they can't keep her here forever, and don't you think the trees in Paris would be beautiful this time of year? All the colours, falling. The perfect place to disappear into.

I shut off my car. Inside, I navigate through the tables to a stool at the bar. At one end, a bunch of white guys—likely construction workers, judging by their orange safety vests—sit in front of beers. Devin sits alone with a dark drink in front of her. Her hair falls over her face like in the photo, but the bump on her nose is visible, even in the dim bar lighting. I hold my breath. If she's back, here, why didn't she come find me? She wouldn't know my new address, but she could have gone to my dad's. Is she mad at me? Upset that I made her so sick? She lifts her drink to her mouth, doesn't glance my way.

I bite the insides of my cheeks. Real pain. Blink. Devin, still on the bar stool, staring at her phone. I slide onto the seat beside her, pretend to consider the different beers on tap. Give her a chance to break the silence first, to explain. But she doesn't say anything, doesn't even look at me. Is she ashamed? Gone for over four years, convinced everyone that she died, even me. What could she say?

As I turn to face her, she stands, doesn't make eye contact, but speaks to me. "Watch my drink for a minute." She turns toward the washroom.

One hand in her pocket, she pushes the door open with her other hand. Two hands, but Devin lost one to the infection. She must've gotten a prosthetic after all.

"Does it . . . How does . . ." I stop, unable to form my question.

"It's weird, not having a hand anymore." Devin holds up both arms between us. "I know it isn't there—I can see that it's gone. But sometimes I'll reach for the remote or my cup and I swear I can still pick things up. Like it's just invisible."

I wave my hand over the empty space where hers should be, hoping to make contact, to link her missing fingers with mine. Nothing. I don't feel any appendages.

"Will you ever get a fake hand to replace it?"

"My doctor says that would help with my phantom syndrome, or whatever this is, but I don't know. Maybe, when I'm sure my hand really is gone."

"ID," the bartender demands, impatient, pulling me from the past.

I open my wallet and take my driver's license from the clear slot, and hand it to him. Been legal for over two years, so I have nothing to hide. Don't need to put in effort for my appearance, either. Devin and I, we used to dress up, even for the liquor store. Lowcut tanks, miniskirts, armed with our fakes and lipstick smiles.

The bartender places my card in front of me, satisfied. "What can I get you?"

"What she's having." I motion with my head to Devin's drink.

Devin returns and finally looks at me as she sits back down. "You look familiar."

I open my mouth to respond, to say "how do you not recognize me?" but she cuts me off.

"You work at a funeral home."

"Uh, yeah, I do. How did you . . . ?"

The bartender deposits a drink in front of me, and I pick it up, sip through the miniature green straw. Sickly sweet with a slight afterburn. Rum and coke.

"You picked up my nan last week. She had an aneurism. We all told her to take it easy, think about retiring, you know? But she refused to listen. Was convinced the Empress hotel couldn't run without her overseeing the catering staff and the maids. Personally, I think they're better off without her breathing down their necks, even if they did organize a *celebration of life* where they all toasted to Nan's memory. I'm Rachelle, by the way." She extends a very real and not-prosthetic hand to shake mine, as her other equally real hand lifts her glass to her lips. Not Devin.

Of course she isn't Devin. Devin did die. No matter how much she schemed about escaping, the infection was too severe, too quick. No chance for her to outrun it.

I copy Rachelle and sip my drink. I still don't know the right words to give someone when a loved one dies.

"You guys did a great job getting her ready. She was always so sharp. Acerbic, really. But somehow, despite the godawful suit, you made her look like a grandma. Soft."

I nod, unwilling to help this woman berate her recently deceased grandmother. People say cruel things when someone dies unexpectedly. As if their loved one chose to leave, to abandon everyone. There's a reason I don't have many photos of Devin, and why Dad keeps boxes of dead people's stuff in his basement. Some of us want to destroy what we had before, and some of us need to keep it, preserved and intact, where time cannot see.

I drink, the rum tasting better. At least, not as overly sweet. Rachelle pulls her phone out again. "Don't you just hate it when your friends are late? How hard is it to send a text with an update— *sorry, I'll be another half hour?*"

"Right?"

I need to leave, get out of here before her friends show up and she introduces me, the part-time mortician-slash-body transporter. They'll ogle me, fascinated by my *profession*, and wonder if my poorly dyed black hair is part of the job, or if I'm an emo-goth girl. Into death metal and hard drugs and leather boots. I wiggle my toes against the soles of my flip flops. So much for stereotypes. I'll disappoint them and then bore them. Anyway, what am I doing here? Did I really think I'd find Devin in a bar on a Thursday afternoon? No, not really. I just wanted to escape, to stop looking at that photo on my phone, to forget for a few hours. She died. Devin died.

APARTMENT

Back home and restless. I want to drive, to copy *No Fixed Address*'s Arachne, and just leave. She didn't leave Vancouver alone, though, she had that guy, Timothy or Thomas, and they had wild sex on the drive. What do I have? One suitcase and a matching carry-on used once, during our trip to Europe, which was really a trip to London-Brighton-Paris and not the whole continent. But we liked the feel of *Europe* in our mouths, how much more culture it implied.

The inside pockets of my suitcase are littered with remnants from that trip, the same month I turned seventeen. It was the best birthday present, travelling with Devin, my dad paying for everything, shuttling us around cottage country sides and fast cities. I pull out the leftover debris. Perfume samples from London. Stones from the beach at Brighton, smooth, grey now, but opalescent when wet. And, impossibly, a photo of Devin and me, Paris. As I searched Dad's place for a photo I failed to destroy, I had this one right here, tucked in the back of my closet the whole time.

We must've gotten one of our disposable cameras developed there—we each had one, and Dad used the digital camera. In this photo, Devin and me, sitting at a round table. Some sort of café. We have miniature Styrofoam cups and a plate of fruit flan. I hold a forkful of flan in front of my mouth, smiling. I could pretend to lose this exact moment among all the other moments we shared, but I know it was morning, across the street from the Louvre, while we waited for the museum to open.

We stopped for breakfast at a small café. Rectangular, long, with a narrow opening and only three tables. The hotel charged twelve Euros for a bowl of cereal, but this café advertised breakfast for five Euros in a small sign on the window. A shot of espresso and slice of pie. We praised ourselves for our delicate sips of the strong coffee and pinky-promised to never leave each other.

I set the photo aside.

Devin never told me she was dying. In the hospital, she kept repeating that she would get out "one way or another," and find me so we could run away together. Could she have escaped? I didn't see her body, just a container full of ashes that everybody claimed was Devin. What was left of her. Fragments of bone. She'd have had to really commit to being dead—leave for almost five years. Get a false identity, a job. Come back when no one expects it. I just have to catch up with her now. Follow her lead. But where would she go?

Suitcase empty, the vestiges from our trip thrown onto my bedroom floor as I reason that Devin must be alive. I assemble a random assortment of clothes and topple them into my suitcase. Jeans, shorts, dresses, sweaters, sequined tanks, scarves. I repack the stones, leave the expired perfume. Our picture rests beside my fingertips. I'm on the left, cheeks bulging from flan and smiling. Devin has her cup in both hands, covering her chin. Her thick hair frames the Styrofoam cup. I don't know why the café didn't serve us real mugs. Maybe they worried we'd break them or steal them, or maybe they had just run out of ceramic mugs and figured a couple of teenagers wouldn't care. The vessels didn't bother us as much as the coffee itself, but by that day, near the end of our trip, we'd gotten used to ordering *"deux cafés, s'il vous plaît,"* and receiving two servings of espresso.

Funny, how I drank espresso five years ago, and now I can barely stomach a vanilla latte, much less regular coffee. Of course, Devin would tell me that my dislike of coffee is actually "a dislike of bad coffee," and that "North Americans don't know how to brew it properly." She spoke like that, as if she didn't belong here, as if she had just returned from a solo soul-searching trip and would let me in on all the secrets she discovered. As if I were worthy. Not that she went anywhere, except that one trip with me and my dad. Still, I would listen, rapt. Would nod and tell myself, yeah, you have taste and this coffee is garbage. Eventually, I became suspicious when I couldn't find any coffee I enjoyed.

Maybe I never liked the espresso—maybe I convinced myself I did to impress Devin. To show her I was cool and smart and sophisticated. Mature.

I leave the photo on my bed and bring my bag to my car, toss it on the back seat. Back in the house I take another walk around. I could have packed up the rest of my stuff, left it at my dad's, but why bother? A plant, laptop, TV, textbooks. Just stuff. Now I don't need to bother cleaning out that pot. Could've called Kramer to tell him I quit, but he'll figure it out. I keep clicking my phone open to stare àt that photo of her, Devin, my Devin. Time to go. Time to find her. No one else believes she's waiting, hoping, to be found. Devin came from Calgary, and so maybe she went back there. Not for stability or a suburban house or even her family, but for the cracks and crevices. Anonymity between familiarity. The places Devin could have seeped into. I pick up the flan-espresso photo and my copy of *No Fixed Address*, and carry them to my car.

I fasten my two pictures from Europe to my car visor with a bulldog clip. Next to the mirror. I don't look anything like her. My eyes are too big, round, my face round too. Devin was always lines, her own lines of flight. Her nose straight until I broke it.

Off the ferry, I drive through spattered lights. Some streetlamps lit, others not yet. That time of dusk when not all light sensors register dark. No pine trees, they've all been cleared for concrete, if they ever even grew here. In my rear view the ocean glints, mirroring the city. Time to drive. I touch the clip clutching my pictures. Goodbye, goodbye.

I walk through the open door. Front counter, two secretaries, nurse's room. Principal and vice-principal's offices hiding down the hall. My dad sits in a chair. One of the chairs usually reserved for delinquents. Elbows on his knees, forehead in hands. Still.

"Devin." He looks up. Red-rimmed eyes. "It spread. Further than they thought. Lungs. Her lungs collapsed."

"But she's okay." I stare at the pine outside the window. It waves at me.

"They couldn't save her."

Blink. Blink away moisture. The pine, focus. The pine stops waving, isn't welcoming. It glows, pulses. Needles vibrate. Black creeps from my peripherals, engulfs. Needles shatter, scatter, pinpricks of light.

Devin always said her city was the sunniest in the world. That even in a blizzard in February the sun played catch with the snowflakes. Since crossing the provincial border, and then, hours later, into her city, all I've seen are trees and rain. Sporadic rain and thin, scraggly trees. No leaves. I breathe the crisp rain through my open window, so different from the Island's heavy humidity. I don't know why we never came here together. It was her city, after all.

I know I can call my Aunt Jocelyn and Uncle Roy and stay with them. But I can't, not really. And, anyway, Devin might come back to her hometown, but she wouldn't go back to the family that sent her away.

My drive through the mountains didn't involve stops at diners or sex with stray men. I went all night, only stopping for gas and a Tim Horton's sandwich in Hope. Not tired, not yet. I can't shake the feeling that if I fall asleep, I'll wake up and remember that Devin isn't alive, that I won't ever catch up with her. As if I was tricked into believing she died, and if I lower my defenses the trick will work all over again. Of course, I know she did die, was cremated. But. She's waiting for me. I just have to figure out where.

Traffic surges around me—morning rush hour. So many cars going nowhere. My head nods on my neck, and I turn up the radio, flick through stations to find one to sing along with. No use, I only find country stations. Need to exit, get off Deerfoot, away from these people. Get walking, or something. A sign indicates that the next exit is for the zoo. Devin talked about it, before. She liked the elephants. Always wanted to go to Africa and see elephants without fences. I suspect Africa has fences too, but I never told her that. She liked to dream of being free.

The park's barely opened for the day, and mostly deserted. The rain continues in a steady sprinkle, turning to mist on the cement walkways. A group of turquoise-clad children and their guards march in front of me and head for the prehistoric section first. I follow them, something about the excited way they point to the statues draws me. Paint peeling, metal rods showing where the raptors and triceratopses are anchored to the ground. But these kids don't see any of that. They shriek as they go around corners and confront looming monsters, teeth bared. I try to imagine creeping back in time. I can't. Devin could've. I leave the children with the dinosaurs and wander through the rest of the zoo.

Eventually the rain stops, but the animals don't come out. I walk around the park, entering and exiting buildings haphazardly, aiming for the elephant enclosure, expecting to see Devin at any moment. Instead of looking for her directly, I try to reassure her, feign interest in the information signs posted outside cages, and wait for her to approach. My eyes, tired, have difficulty focusing on the words and images describing the different animals. A sign on the elephant enclosure says they're from Asia, and I don't immediately realize that there aren't also African elephants.

I decide to sit halfway up the bleachers. Still no elephants outside. A few people jostle each other at the food vendor stall behind me. Can't see any animals, can only hear people ordering the hungry lion poutine. I pull my hair back into a French braid that twists from my right temple to rest over my left shoulder. Streaks of black dye stain my fingertips. I don't know how long I watch the empty enclosure. The elephants are inside. I see an entrance to go look at them in the big domed building. But Devin wouldn't go inside, into another confined space.

I wish I'd thought to bring my book with me, but it's on the back seat of my car. Could have flipped through the pages and followed Arachne's journey, and waited for Devin to sit beside me and say: "Finally got around to reading *No Fixed Address*?" in her teasing way that makes me a little defensive. And I'd pretend like I'd read it before—cobble together an opinion based off the lectures I've attended. She'd see right through me. Call me "liar" to my face, and then we'd both laugh because we'd know she was right.

"Coffee?" A small girl wearing a leopard print headband and bright blue polo shirt, a cup in each hand, stands beside me. For a moment I think she's Devin, conjured to me, but the moment passes quickly. Her name tag hangs askew, like she pinned it in a rush before work. Keelie. Too short to be Devin. And too old— Keelie has fine lines around her eyes, on her forehead.

"Do I know you?" I ask.

A breeze tugs stray strands from her messy bun. "You look cold."

"The sun's out."

"Your hair's still wet. Coffee?"

"Thanks." Maybe she pities me, but my fingers need something warm to hold on to.

"I'm Keelie. There's only milk in the coffee. That's how I like it." She passes me a cup, paper, with a tiger's face, teeth clenched, printed on one side, and sits next to me.

"What a coincidence, me too." Well, that's how I take my tea. "I'm Rachelle." I smile at her and slide over on the bench so she can sit with me.

She sits and sips her coffee. "Where're you from?"

"How do you know I'm not from here?"

"Hard to find a born-and-raised Calgarian still in the city."

Kids shriek and run around us, arms outstretched, impervious to the disappointment of an empty cage. One jumps in a nearby puddle and splashes Keelie's pants.

"Fucking great." She swipes at her leg but doesn't manage to remove any mud. "The children should be caged, or leashed, at the very least." She rolls her eyes and grins. Sounds like she's said this before, probably every couple of shifts.

"Were you?" I sip the coffee. The milk makes it drinkable, but only barely. Less bitter, but weirdly thin. Closer to tea, but not as comforting.

Keelie looks at me questioningly.

"Born here? Or a transplant from another city?" I clarify.

She nods with her coffee at her mouth. "All twenty-seven years I've been alive. Never even travelled anywhere."

I nod to myself—I knew she was too old to be Devin in disguise. Anyway, Devin wouldn't disguise herself around me. "Devin, my cousin, was like that, but then she came and lived with me for a bit, and we went to Europe for a few weeks."

"Europe? That's fascinating. I've always wanted to go to Venice or Toulouse. Prague. Amsterdam. Ugh, so many places!"

The sun's getting hotter as it gets lower, or maybe the coffee's warming me from the inside. My stomach gurgles, grateful to receive some amount of sustenance. Should've eaten earlier.

Distracted, I reply after a long of a pause. "We went all over Britain's countryside, stopping in small towns where the cottages are named things like *Thorneberry Villa* and *Evergreen Copse*. And we went to Paris."

"Paris. Is it really as amazing as everyone says?" Keelie perks up, her gaze intent on my face—a city girl, the kind enamoured with building lights at night, and bars with live music.

Devin was, too. Maybe that's the effect of this city.

"I don't speak French," I answer, to avoid telling her what it was really like. I can't give up Devin, our stories, not so easily.

"I don't either."

We watch the empty enclosure, sipping our bland and tepid coffee. She's more comfortable with silence. I spin my cup, in my hands, around. Around. I jiggle my legs, cross my ankles, uncross them. Is she on break or off shift? Why is she still sitting with me?

"You've lived here your whole life, right?" I turn to Keelie.

"Yeah. That's what I told you." She tosses her empty cup in the bin beside the bleachers.

"Did you know Devin?"

"Devin?"

"Evans. Here, this is what she looked like." I left my glossy photos on my car visor, but I pull out my cell and open my saved image.

"That's so cool your cousin's a model for the She's Not Dead campaign!"

"Oh?" Startled. What does she know about this, about what Devin's doing?

"Yeah. MADD Canada's doing a great job with these ads. Have you seen the one with the guy in the wheelchair? Or the one about the father who can't read to his kid anymore because of brain damage? They're only using actual survivors, or so I hear. Was your cousin one of the drunk drivers that killed someone? Oh my god, I'm so sorry, don't answer, I didn't mean for that to come out!"

I blink, taken aback. Devin was in an accident? Did she cause the accident, or was she jaywalking and got hit? She wouldn't be so irresponsible as to drink and drive unless there was no other choice. She must've been hit by someone else—she never liked the confines of crosswalks. Does she have amnesia? Brain damage? After her amputation and everything else, then her memories. Pieces of her taken away. Missing.

"Who knows, maybe the *real survivors* thing is bullshit. She could've just gone to a photoshoot."

"No, no. She was jaywalking and got hit. Memory loss. She forgets where she is, who she is, forgets the people who love her. That's why I have to find her."

The elephant's enclosure is still empty. If Devin's forgotten herself, maybe she is inside, after all. Or maybe she doesn't recognize me, won't be able to find me.

"Oh, I'm so sorry." Keelie bites her lip. "I don't know if this would help, but I'm having a party, well, me and my roommates. And there'll be a lot of people. You could come, ask around?"

I mimic Keelie and throw my cup at the bin. It skids over the far edge and rolls underneath. Devin loves parties—even if she has brain damage, she could turn up. And Rachelle wouldn't miss an opportunity to party.

"Yeah, actually. That's a good idea."

No one walks around near us. The park is quiet. Keelie adds her number to my phone and enters her address into my Google Maps app.

"Come by any time after eight. Music's at ten, so you can ask about her before everyone's hammered." She smiles at me and stands. "Park's closed now, so we should probably go."

"I will. Just give me minute?" I stand and move closer to the enclosure. Put my hands on the metal railing, still cold despite the sun.

Keelie stretches, and her shirt untucks itself. "Okay, see you tonight." Waves as she walks away.

An elephant emerges from the darkened doorway, swinging its trunk. Another follows. Somehow, they move silently. Their huge bodies amble toward me, seeming so light. Almost as if they aren't present.

"Hey, we're closed. You have to head to the exit."

I turn to a man in a security uniform. He's got his hands on his hips. No nonsense.

"Yes, sir. Sorry, I didn't know."

Spinning around, I don't see Devin. Time to look elsewhere.

The police picked me up from a house party. I'd snuck out of Dad's from the basement window—the screen pops out easily, and for some reason none of the basement windows are alarmed. No beeping on the security system. Not that he sets it often.

I was smoking outside the house, a whole group of us were. Kids from school, and their older siblings and their friends. We liked them. The older kids, adults, really. They brought cheap vodka and handfuls of pills. Ecstasy, probably. Maybe something else. We could get weed ourselves.

Sitting in the station, in a chair in an empty hallway, I try to tell them my side of the story: "Someone drugged me. Slipped something in my drink. I thought it was him."

Him, the guy, the one burned by my lit cigarette. The one who hit me. The one I pushed into the grass where a small fire started from my fallen cigarette. "Lucky his fall smothered the fire and only wrecked his jeans. No permanent damage." That's what the cop told me happened. I listened, eyes closed. That's not what happened. I didn't notice the fire. I didn't know. I swear. I didn't mean it.

"We have witnesses that saw you willingly take drugs."

"They're lying. Liars. No. That didn't happen."

I can't get the cop to focus. Into focus. His uniform blurry, and I vomit between my legs. All liquid. It comes out my nose, my eyes burn. My pants are wet.

Footsteps, and my dad's voice, but I can't really hear. Just sounds. Shapes of words through the buzzing in my mind. Another voice. Angry. They're always angry with me. No, not me. The cop leaves.

"If you think that's best." Dad talks to the angry voice.

His hand pushes my damp bangs off my forehead. Massages my neck. Someone shoves paper towel, rough, the bargain brand like at the school, they rub my face. Wipe my chin clean. A plastic cup of water in my hand.

"Home?" I croak, not looking at him. Not able to raise my head to look.

"Not yet, sweetie. You're going to the doctor first."

The lawn has a big, wooden sign baring the name *Home on the Range* just above the house number. It looks like the type of sign that belongs in front of an acreage or ranch, not a normal house on a residential street close to the university. On the front door a note scribbled on lined paper asks partiers to "please enter through back," with an arrow pointing to the side of the house. Painted on a rock placed to block the front door from being opened are the words "we're all mad here," and an image of a girl in a blue dress, surrounded by giant mushrooms with spots in pink, purple, and green. Maybe the lawn sign isn't so out of place.

I follow the directions on the door to a gate that leads to the backyard. Keelie stands with a group of six people clustered between the detached garage and back door. Cigarettes in everyone's hands or mouths. I extract one from my purse as I join the circle.

"Here." A boy with long dreads whips out a zippo, swipes it on his leg to light it, and holds the flame for me.

I inhale. "Thanks." Blow smoke at his face. It gets lost in his hair.

"One day that move'll get you laid. Probably not tonight though." Keelie laughs as she plucks the lighter from his hand and uses it.

"I can always try, Kee."

"Clive, this is Rachelle."

"Elle." I go for a handshake, but he pulls me in for a hug. I hold my cigarette awkwardly, trying not to touch his hair or back. Don't want to start another fire.

Clive releases me. "We're huggers here. Hope you don't mind."

"Not at all."

Keelie only smokes half her cigarette, pinches the cherry off, and puts the remainder in her pack.

"I'll be back, just going to check if they're almost ready."

"Who?" I ask, but she's already inside.

"The band. First up is Zackariah and The Prophets, then All Hands on Jane, and Dead Pretty. Then me." Clive answers.

"You're in a band?"

"No. I DJ."

"That's cool." I inhale a long drag.

The yard extends to the end of the garage and backs onto an alleyway. People stand in pockets, leaning against the fence, the garage, a circle around a large firepit. They take turns tossing sticks and leaves in handfuls into the flames. All the cigarettes, joints, the fire, they cast a haze that blends into the greying sky. Night seems to roll in on the smoke.

"This lineup is fucking insane!" A girl, her face painted in black swirls and sparkles, exclaims and my attention is drawn back to the conversation around me.

"You play?" I ask.

"Drums with Dead Pretty. I'm Pigeon."

"Elle."

"Cool, see you in there." She throws her stub at the ashtray, misses, picks it up, and places it in the jar of butts, then goes inside.

I turn to Clive, but he's engrossed in a discussion about geometric shapes and the dimensions of the universe with another long-haired white guy. I'm too sober for any theoretical conversation. Some chairs and blue coolers are arranged in an attempted circle a little outside the ring around the firepit, and I meander toward them. A white plastic chair, spray painted with flecks of green and yellow, sits between an overturned milk crate and a greenhouse. I slide onto the flowered seat.

"Cheers!" the guy on the milk crate twists, a beer in his hand, huge smile.

"Cheers!" I reply, fist-bumping his beer can.

"No drink?"

I didn't bring any. Didn't think to stop at a liquor store earlier. "Not yet."

"We can't have that! Here, hope you like Lucky." He passes me a can from a case beside him.

I crack it open. "Thanks."

"No worries, lovely lady. You need to give if you have. Even if you don't have, you still need to give. Eventually everything comes back. But you might need to ask."

"So true, man!" A shirtless guy with an impressive ginger beard leans across the circle. "I didn't have any smokes on me, asked this fellow here for one, and he gives me a pack."

"I know you'll get me back someday, or someone else will. Probably already has."

A guest comes in for group talks every Wednesday evening. Someone who went through "the program," as they call it. Tonight, Annabelle tells us, "It's okay, people need to be able to give and receive. You especially need to receive right now. Just breathe in all the love and support of your families, and when you're better you'll be ready to give again." As if we're here because we gave too much love away, as if love corresponds to sanity, and innocuous pills taken at prescribed times will make up for our lack of love and teach us that *drugs are bad.*

As if love or its lack have anything to do with why I am here. But the group therapy was a compromise. No community service, no drug rehab. The doctors and the social worker and the police, none of them could agree where I belonged. They sent me to the psych ward for a bit, but that wasn't quite right. The social worker, Mrs. Elba, "but please call me Lana," who chewed out the cop who picked me up, she said that "normal teenage outbursts often appear as psychotic behaviours, especially when coupled with drug use." So there. Nothing wrong with me. And the guy, well, only his pride was actually injured. He didn't press charges, probably because he didn't want to admit to "sharing" drugs with "children." The law and the medical communities, for once in agreement, insistent on seeing me as a kid.

I pretended not to listen to the counsellors and guest speakers, but later I tell Devin the same thing, tell her she needs to receive love, when she's in the hospital, different hospital, different reason. She laughs at me, asks if I was forced to read self-help books. But when I get up to leave, she squeezes my hand, just a little.

Drums reverberate, thump, thud. And a deep boom, boom, booming in the background, clawing under my skin, settling in my pelvis and escaping through my mouth in gasps and shouts with the crowd. Cymbals crash under Pigeon's blonde hair, light shines, reflects her painted swirls. Keelie dances beside me. Every part of her moving. Shoulders and hands pumping, back and forth. Back and forth. Head twisting, mouth open, screaming along with the singer. Words lost between the drumbeat and bass. Knees bending, curving out. Toes rolling, stamping. I catch her eye, try to match her pulse. She grabs my wrists, twirls me around. Around around around around.

Around and she lets me go, dances with another girl. They shimmy down, pull each other up. I bang my head on the air. Boom. Boom. Between the lights and sound, I watch Pigeon. Pounding. Drumsticks on every drum at once. Cymbal. Cymbal. Stop. Her small hands hold the metal still. She looks up. At me. I vibrate, my ribs quiver, arms up. Jump jump jump.

After their set I cross the duct taped line that marks the stage, offer my praise, hope for a touch from Pigeon's hand. Her hands so strong. Almost violent. I'm standing beside one of her drums, not the big one. She's talking to a guy who got to her first, and the guitarist. No one's saying anything, just "good job," and "that went really well."

"Rachelle! Have you met everyone?" Keelie slips an arm under my elbow, around my waist.

"Elle. I like Elle better."

"Sweet. This is Pigeon, Kris, and Shayla."

I wave at the other two. "We've met." I smile at Pigeon. Lips only, one side of my mouth pulls further back than the other.

"Good. Wonderful people like you should meet each other!"

"Everyone is wonderful people." A tall guy with a scarf tied as a skirt comes behind Keelie and tangles her in his long arms.

I dance my way to the back yard, find another beer in a case in the garden. Sit on a tree stump in front of the fire. A few people lounge on other stumps or concrete lumps or lawn chairs. Warmth over my chest, and I realize I lost my shirt. That's right, on the dance floor. Most of the people around the fire have lost their shirts or pants. Bras too, they litter the ground between beer cans. I check—still wearing mine. Smoke a cigarette and puff a joint someone passes through the circle. It's mellow. The fire flares at the centre of the circle. People dissipate over time, go to the garage or back to the house. My head droops forward. Eyes close. Music still plays across my mind, looping and crashing in a sleep-muffled track.

I haven't passed around Devin's photo, haven't asked about her. Even almost forgot about her as I watched Pigeon play her drums. Felt her beat a rhythm into my muscles.

As if summoned by my thoughts, Pigeon sits on the grass beside me. "Elle."

I open my eyes to a lightening sky, find her face. "Pigeon." Her sparkles dance in the dying firelight. We are alone outside.

Her eyes mark my body, as if creating glimmering tracks over my skin. "I like the taste of your name." Fingers find the curve behind my knee.

"Nice line."

Backlit by daybreak, I can't see her features, just her outline against the fire's gasping embers. Smoke wafts upward, obscures the clouds. Grey over grey over grey. Pigeon pulls my attention back to her by releasing my hair from its braid.

She leans over for a kiss, I move toward her, but don't line up quite right and her lips get the spot beside my nose. I laugh as I fall off my stump. Roll over so my stomach presses into the broken sidewalk stone. Grass, thick from all the rain, pricks into my exposed skin. Pull a sweater or a scarf under my torso. Somebody else's clothes strewn over the backyard serve as a makeshift blanket.

Pigeon tickles my back, then flips me over again, using her hands and leg so when I'm on my back, she straddles my hips. No pants, no underwear. I reach up, find her nipples under her loose shirt. Pinch them, rub circles larger and larger around until they're hard under my palms. She pulls away, but only to move farther down. Edging my pants down and legs apart, she ducks her head and I feel her tongue. I bunch my hands in her long hair and notice she has a shaved patch above her right ear. I'm panting, moaning. And. And her teeth graze my thighs, nose on my clit. Tongue inside, gentle, gentle, then two fingers inside me.

"Oh, oh, ohhhh."

"Shhh."

My body convulses, hips thrust, beg her to go deeper. Can't control. I'm a taut skin vibrating, writhing from her hands and I'm sure that this is music.

Pigeon drags her tongue over my belly button. Ears tingling inside, not quite ringing. Legs shaking but unable to move. I pull her face to me, kiss her, take her tongue, scrape my teeth along the top.

She jerks back, spits at the ground, but hits my arm. Her saliva's dark. The same dark dribbles over her chin. Pigeon spits again. Still dark.

"You bit me."

I don't remember biting her. I don't remember anything. My legs won't move.

I thought I'd leave this city. Look for Devin elsewhere. Where? I drive around Calgary. Southbound Deerfoot until I pass the city limits sign and hit Okotoks. I swing around. Back onto Deerfoot, this time northbound. Then I exit onto Glenmore, pass the huge mall, and take the exit for Crowchild. Devin always talked about Kensington and the coffee place there. The Rotisserie. No, not a chicken place. I can't leave until I go there. I remember she used to tease me, saying she wouldn't take me until I appreciated good coffee, because I had to try the New Orleans blend. Someone mentioned the place at the party, making plans to meet in Kensington, drink coffee. I can barely stand coffee even when it's loaded with milk or frothed with cream and vanilla syrup, but, just for Devin, I'll go try a cup her way. If I don't like this coffee, then I'll know for sure that I don't like coffee, not that I have superior tastes and can only enjoy premium brews.

I park on the street and pay at an electronic meter on the corner. Enter my licence plate and insert my credit card. No idea how long I'll be, so I opt for two hours, then wander down the block in search of Devin's café. Pass a crystal shop and bookstore, but don't go in. I get to the end of the street where the river gushes beneath a bridge leading to downtown. Behind me is a coffee place, but it doesn't have the right name. And a tea place. But Devin hates tea—she thinks it's a weak imitation.

I walk back, try the other way down the street from where I parked. Under a yellow awning, I find a sign proclaiming *The Roasterie* in green semi-cursive. That's it. People stand outside smoking, and I recognize Clive. I raise my hand and walk over. Before I can fish out a cigarette, Clive passes me one and lights his zippo. Using his thumb, not thigh. Guess he's not interested in me anymore.

"Thanks. How's it going?" I look at the other people in this circle. Two guys who could be twins, both wearing aviators and pinstriped pants. A girl with four lip piercings and a pink flower in her hair. No Keelie. No Pigeon.

"Good. How about you?"

"All right. Glad I found this place."

A guy with a guitar sits on the stone outline of the dilapidated flower patch beside us and starts strumming. An upside-down toque beside his foot. The group is silent, like I've interrupted their conversation. Like they don't want me around.

I persist, remember I need to ask about Devin and the black-and-white ad with the weird caption. "A friend told me it's the only place for a good cup of coffee."

"Smart friend." The pierced girl places her hand on Clive's upper arm.

"She is, even with the memory loss. Do you know her? Devin Evans."

Clive takes a long drag and the ash builds on the end of his cigarette. "Devin Evans? Did someone seriously give their kid a rhyming name?"

I ignore his comment. "Here, I have a picture." I open the photo on my phone and turn it to the group.

The guitarist starts singing a song I don't recognize. People walking by drop coins into his hat with a faint clink. He doesn't interrupt his song to say thanks.

"Hard to see her face." Pierced girl leans over to look. "Isn't that from the anti-drug campaign? I thought you said she was cool."

"Anti-drugs?" I look back at Devin on my phone. Wasn't this for Mothers Against Drunk Driving? Memory loss and brain damage, and how she forgot how to find me?

"Yeah, our asshole conservative government," One of pinstriped twins sucks his cigarette before finishing his thought. "They're running this thing about how drugs turn you into prostitutes. How she's not dead, but just sucking the taxpayers' resources for healthcare. It's all bullshit, really."

I smile. She didn't forget me. She's just stuck without money, without a way to get to me.

The other aviatored guy drops his butt in the old coffee-cannister-turned-ashtray. "What, you think that's a good thing? Next you know we'll have privatized healthcare that no one can afford. People are still people, still human beings. Don't matter what they do to get by."

"No. I mean, yes. I agree. Sorry." I shake my head and pull out my picture of us in Paris. "I'm just trying to find her. Have you guys seen her?" I hand the picture to Clive.

"Oh yeah, her." He lights another cigarette. "I guess her name was Devin. Yeah, she was here a lot. We used to talk."

"About?"

Pierced girl takes the photo. "Damn, that was a long time ago. Totally forgot about her."

The matching guys nod as the photo is passed around and makes it back to me. I can't tell if the guitarist behind our little circle is still playing the same song or a new one.

"Poetry, mostly." Clive inhales, his eyes focused above me, like he's thinking. "And travel, she wanted a car to drive down to Nelson, but everyone here wants to go to Nelson. What happened to her? She hasn't been around."

"We lived together on the Island for a bit. But I'm trying to find out where she went from there." I tuck the photo back into my pocket.

"Good luck." Clive says, and I recognize that he doesn't want to talk about this anymore.

I walk to the door, and the group continues its conversation about politics, how for a government that doesn't believe in big government, they sure have their hands in everyone's pockets, noses in everyone's business. The warm coffee smell greets me like steam from a sauna. I order a New Orleans blend from the short guy with a fedora.

"Great choice. You know, I love this blend. I have a cup before bed, every night. Make it half strength and it tastes just like tea. But better, because it's coffee. You want it to go?"

"Yeah, I've got to get back to work." Back to finding Devin.

"In Grade 12, I gave up sex. For a while. Met some hippies, bohemians, who were all about sharing the love. I went to poetry readings." Devin leans over my dresser, close to the mirror, as she swipes black eyeliner along her bottom rim.

"Oh, god, I can only imagine. Scrawny white guys crooning about lost love through abstract metaphors." I roll my eyes.

"No, well, yes, but there's always free wine at poetry events, and some of it was good."

I flip through my homework. Don't bother asking about underage drinking—I know she has a fake, and it seems like people in Calgary barely ID pretty girls with tits. Instead, I proclaim: "Poetry sucks. We're supposed to *extract meaning* and the *real issue* from a bunch of jumbled words. I don't even think half of these poets meant for their work to be interpreted in a *deeper cultural and literary context.*"

"You can't be taught poetry." Devin states, standing upright with her hands on her bare hips, wearing short-shorts and a bra.

I try to raise one eyebrow at her and fail. She laughs.

"Poetry, good poetry, should be like an acid trip. Hilarious, terrifying, take you outside yourself so you see the interlocking bricks of words as sound, and take you so deep inside you start to doubt you're your body."

I toss my homework over the edge of my bed. What I wouldn't give to have graduated already, like Devin. At least she doesn't find the two-year age difference a problem.

"Poetry is the reason I first took acid," she says.

Devin wasn't with the hippies, maybe she came back to this bar. To forgive, except that she never forgives. To confront, then. The bar doesn't look like the sort of place where girls get roofied. Nice tables and booths, lots of windows, and a small stage for live sets on weekends.

"Is Collin working?" I ask before sitting, before being greeted.

The waitress gives me a blank look.

"Collin. Bartender, scruffy almost beard, wide shoulders, ladies' man."

Another waitress overhears, comes to stand beside the first. "He quit three years ago. Last I heard he was a rig pig up near Edberg."

I sit at the bar anyway. Tell the girl behind the counter to make me anything and to make it strong. She gives me something lime green and blended, not a mojito, but close. I down it all at once and go to the bathroom. Find a stall. Spread myself across the tiled floor. Dirt ground over the grout. Dirt and other shit. Rest my cheek on the cold bowl of a toilet. Heave my stomach so I feel my ribs pinching inwards, and vomit the drink. Neon and burning in my nostrils, behind my eyes, out my tear ducts. Stomach acid and bile and lime scalding my skin.

Devin, Devin! But she doesn't hear me. She doesn't comfort me.

DEERFOOT

In my car, window down, cigarette in hand. I inhale. In. Deeper, deeper. Try to let it, out but forget how, and start to swallow. I cough the smoke out, eyes and ears streaming. Coughs wrack my chest, pound me down onto the steering wheel.

One more stop before I go. A hair salon. I walk in, a boy sits at the front desk, a few years younger than me. High school aged, a fringe of hair over his face, both sides cut short, a design of shooting stars shaved into the left side.

"Hi, do you have an appointment?" Chipper, polite.

I bite my pinkie nail. "No, is that a problem?"

"Nope, not at all. Just a cut??"

"Can you fit me in for a dye too?"

He glances at a calendar in front of him.

"Not today, I can schedule you for one next week though."

"No, it's fine. I just want this patch shaved then," I gesture to the spot above my ear.

"Yeah, for sure. Missy!" he calls over his shoulder, "I got someone for you!"

A girl straightening her hair at the back of the shop glances at us, finishes her bangs and comes over. "Hi, what can I do you for?"

"She said she wanted a patch shaved right about here," the boy demonstrates on himself.

"Sweet, no problem. Want to come back for a wash?"

I weave behind her, passed the rows of mirrors, the stations filled with other people and hairdressers, to the sinks, padded chairs low to the ground with arms reaching further than usual chairs.

My head back, I close my eyes and feel the water push against my scalp. Missy's hands join the water and firmly apply shampoo.

"I just love your colour!"

"Really?" I'm sure she doesn't. It's a shitty box dye, unevenly applied.

Her fingers and palms rub behind my ears and under my hair.

"It's the right sort of dark. Not blueish black, but definitely not natural brown. A hard colour to manage." She rinses the soap out.

"It's not really me, though. I might go blonde again."

With my eyes closed, I can almost imagine Devin sitting in the next chair over, giving me a hard time for my relapse into emo: "It's almost like I had absolutely no impact on you. Your style, at least. And what is this shaved patch all about? You're always trying to be somebody else."

I've been listening to the same CD for over an hour. A mix Devin made for me when I was sick. Usually I drive in silence, turn on the radio only when I have passengers—living or dead—or if I'm trying to stay awake, but tonight my thoughts beat like caged birds against the insides of my ears. Flapping. Pecking. I need the distraction, and I'm too far away from everything for the radio. But this CD wasn't a good choice, because I had strep throat when Devin made it, and she had a torn hangnail.

I meant to head west. Toward Nelson, back to Devin. But I couldn't. Listening to this CD. Her missing arm. Her collapsed lungs. Hospital pudding cups and blue Gatorade. And she still fucking helped me with my homework, listened to me whine about kids at school. What did any of that shit matter when she was dying? Of course, she didn't tell me when she escaped. Of course she left me. Why would she have wanted me to go with her?

Maybe I should run away, like she did. But not in the same direction. Maybe I should let her find me. If she wants to.

No streetlamps out here. Road slick with night blurring the yellow center line into the mark of a highlighter run over wet ink. But there are no words on this highway. Speed limit signs posted on the side of the road the closest to language: *110km/hr.* Other signs depict a white triangle, a man and a woman stick figure separated by a line, or the image of a seatbelt, black and buckled.

No real words. Nothing talking. Just flat asphalt stuck in the middle of flat plains, mountains only an idea at this point. Of course, that's not true. This close to Calgary, the mountains are always present.

Narrow highways are not made for U-turns. Seems obvious, but I didn't realize the non-existent width of this road when I tried to turn around. I blame the dusk and my shitty headlights. But I guess the why and how don't really matter, as I'm stuck in a wheat field, stalks tapping my windows. Great. Wonderful, even. I put my car in reverse, stomp on the gas. The tires make a hissing whine. Or maybe it's the engine. Either way, I'm not going anywhere. The last grey dregs followed the sun downward hours ago. I punch the volume button to turn off the music. Give me some space to think. I could just stay here, for the night. Save me looking for a place to stay in whatever random small town I come across next.

I force my door open, flattening some bristles of wheat while others lash back at me. I step out and lose my feet in hidden snow. Fucking great. Leaving my door open so the light in my car pours out, I wade to my back door behind the passenger seat and hoist my suitcase. I collapse on top of it, take a couple of deep breaths before getting up again. Now to drag this to the front.

"Having fun?"

I turn, cracking my neck. A pick-up, headlights on, grins at me. The driver stands in front of the two beams, only a dark outline. Didn't even hear it approach.

"Tons." I call back, straightening.

"What're you doing out here?"

"I thought this looked like a great place to stay for the night. Nice view and all."

"You aren't going to think that in the morning."

Snow seeps through my sneakers, into my socks. I shuffle my weight between my feet, wiggle my toes. "Why's that?"

"Most farmers around here aren't pleased to find ditzy blondes camped on ruined crop."

"I'm not blonde." The salon didn't have time to re-dye my hair.

"Okay, I'll leave you to sleep then." He turns back to his truck. A souped-up monstrosity, body suspended over the tires, paint shining even without light.

I open my passenger door and fling my suitcase inside. The back seat'll be cramped, but I can make it through one night. A breeze whips the stalks against my waist. I have a blanket in my trunk, but no pillow.

"Unless you want a tow?"

I jolt. Was sure he'd already driven off as silently as he'd arrived. I slam my car door and traipse through the plants back to the driver's side. The guy waits with his arms folded in front of him, leaning against the front of his beast.

"Are you trying to take advantage of me?"

He laughs, deep. Not a short bark. His rolling mirth engulfs me, and we both laugh until our sides heave and we can't take a full breath.

"No, miss. I'm just an honest guy with a truck, asking if you need help."

"Sure you are." I laugh. "Yes. Fine."

"All right, let me string this up. You can get in the driver's seat—not like you'll tip the scales too much. Feel free to lock the doors if you don't trust me." I can't see his face, but I'm sure he's grinning. Can hear it in his voice.

I don't have to do any of the work? Sweet. "Okay." Plonk down into my seat.

I do lock my doors, but I unroll the window all the way and light a cigarette.

"I'm going to tie a rope to the back." He calls, closer now.

"Thanks."

The wheat bristles as my smoke hits it, as if more affronted by the vapours than being crushed under my tires.

"So, where're you headed?"

I shrug, then realize he can't see me from behind. "Not sure."

"Want to follow me back to Forestburg? I doubt you'll be able to find anywhere open to spend the night, but in the morning there's a couple of bed and breakfasts you can check into, or else get a meal at a diner."

"Ah, so that's how you'll lure me into a trap. Offer food and coffee, the possibility of sleep." I tap my ash out the window.

"Damn, you caught onto my plan too quickly. Perhaps I'll have to have my way with you here and now." He moves to the front of my car, rests his forearm over the top of my car door, and leans down, toward my face.

Hair, not long, but in need of a trim, falls over his eyes, his smile is all teeth. I blow smoke at him, and he reaches for me. No, not for me. He plucks my cigarette from my fingers, takes a drag, and gives it back.

"Thanks." He slaps my car door and walks to the back.

HANK'S BISTRO

"Pigeon, how do you find yourself in the middle of Alberta with no idea of where you're going?" Carson adds cinnamon to his coffee. He had to ask the waitress to bring him a shaker.

"How do you come across someone stranded in the middle of Alberta?" I chew at a hangnail on my index finger.

Carson sits with both his elbows on the table. "I was on my way back from a job."

"In the middle of the night?" I don't know how Pigeon takes her coffee, so I add cinnamon to mine as well. She is the girl with swirls on her face and a shaved patch on her head.

"Wasn't the middle of the night." Pause. "I work with cars. I was driving back from a job."

"Isn't it hard to see when it's dark out?"

"You don't know where I was working, where I was coming from." He breaks eye contact to contemplate the laminated menu.

"Well, you could tell me."

Carson laughs. "You're precious."

I look around the diner. A small place, quaint. Just a rectangular room, counter across the back with a single till, booths along the windows and tables scattered in the center. The chairs have metal legs with anti-scuff pads duct taped to the bottoms. Or maybe it's all duct tape. Our booth seat is that not-quite-plastic material used on buses. There's a tear by my left thigh, and I keep sticking my finger through it. In and out, in and out. My doubt from yesterday has vanished. It's like the universe or some bullshit wanted me to turn around, continue my search for Devin. Why else would my car have gotten stuck, and this stranger have offered to help? Maybe he even knows her.

"I'm looking for this girl." I retrieve my Paris photo from my pocket and open the black and white image on my phone. Push them across the table.

"Who is she?" Carson looks at them together.

I sip my coffee. The cinnamon gives it dimension—more flavour, like chai tea. At least, it almost masks the flat, stale taste of small-town diner coffee. I reach across the table for the plastic portions of half-and-half and paper squares of sweetener.

"Devin." I answer as I begin opening packages to dump into my coffee.

"Your sister?" He looks closer at my phone. "What's with the caption?"

"Cousin, sort of. And I don't know. Everyone has a different idea. AIDS awareness, anti-drunk driving, anti-prostitution. Who knows what else?"

"You don't even know what she's up to or who she models for?" Carson pushes my phone and photo across the scratched table, back to me. "And you're what? Just driving around aimlessly hoping to find her?"

I cross my arms, defensive. "I'm going to Nelson."

"Need a second driver?"

Stir my coffee with a plastic stir stick and slurp some. Too much sweetener. The label lied—it is not a sugar substitute that "tastes like the real thing!" Grainy and fake, it makes my coffee taste like a low-calorie diet coke ice cream float without the fizz.

Carson's inside some sort of farmhouse. Or maybe a barn. The two white buildings look identical except that the one Carson entered is slightly smaller. We drove separate cars, me following him. Said he had to leave the truck with his friend. He didn't invite me in, and I didn't want to follow, so I'm waiting in my car for him. I could just leave him here, continue my search on my own. But, without someone else around, a witness, would I continue my search?

Arachne doesn't need anyone to accompany her, but she has her friend Thena as a witness, a co-conspirator, in a way. Someone to receive her stories and egg her on, even if this encouragement is disguised as cautionary warnings. I need someone to keep me going, not to bring me back home. Someone who won't keep insisting that Devin is dead. Someone who believes me.

I don't know how long it's been since I set out. Days blend together and separate. One day could last for three, or a week could be a day. I stare at the black-and-white image on my phone. Dismiss my notifications. I've been avoiding my calls and messages. Mostly from Dad, but a few from Kramer, Rae. It's probably exam break now. Devin, her shoulder raised, looks halfway through a shrug, as if she's just asked me if any of it really matters. I love you, that matters. And, I guess, Dad loves me.

Guilty for a moment, I press his name in my contacts and listen to the dial tone. Five rings. My dad doesn't answer, and I don't talk to his machine. I'll try again later.

I pull out my book. Classes are over, but I still feel like I should finish it. For my mom that I didn't know or for Devin or maybe even for my dad. Arachne's driving around here, too, spiralling east, not west. My journey's not an amorous one, not like hers, and I know I'm not Arachne. That's one thing I know. And I'm not Rachelle or Elle or even Pigeon.

I chew my hangnail while reading.

Carson returns, tosses a bag on the backseat and slams the door. He folds himself into the passenger seat, knees up. Doesn't comment on my cramped car. I tuck my book under a blanket on the backseat. No one else around, not Carson's so-called business partners, or even a bird. Blue skies and bare land, a dusting of snow from last night.

"Where are we headed?" I ask, my fingers tapping the steering wheel.

"Where do you want to go?" He's focused on the side of his seat, probably trying to locate the mechanism to slide himself back.

He finds a lever, pulls it, and the seat flattens backward, headrest touching the backseat. Carson struggles to return to a sitting position.

"Here, it's in the front." I reach between his awkwardly scrunched legs and lift the rod to give him more leg room.

"Thanks."

"I thought you worked with cars."

"I'm not usually in the passenger seat." He pushes his hair off his face.

"I don't usually drive living people, but here we are."

Carson says he wants to make one more stop before we leave. Not about business. I pull over beside the sidewalk adjacent to the cemetery gate. This place is too small for anyone to mind. The gates, black wrought iron, as cemetery gates should be, refuse to be intimidating or benevolent. They simply stand there, waiting, prickly grass growing at their feet, as if neither will die, as if both have been there forever.

A path leads from the gates straight back, just a gravel path, icy, with a thin layer of snow over top, gravestones on either side. Unassuming, square or rectangular stones, a name, two dates, and sometimes an inscription. No one here died wishing to be noticed. Only love would bring visitors here. I don't belong. An onlooker, watching Carson ahead, legs shoulder-width apart in front of a pale stone. Arms straight by his sides, fingers tapping his knees. I step closer to the stones on my left, away from Carson. No unearthed skull or old man appears.

I go back to my car, whisper the pads of my fingers over the steering wheel, dash, emergency brake.

This is my car. Not Pigeon's. I pull her long hair over my face, feel the strands as sandpaper against my cheeks, smoothing away my features. I have freckles, Pigeon doesn't.

Can I carve colours out of my skin, gouge out the specks one by one with my pinkie nail, cleaning the unwanted by running my tooth along the underside of my nail? Carson might come back before I'm done, and then what? Would I look crazy, car visor down to expose a mirror, divots in my face filling with red? Hair still across my face, thin lines blurring my sight, obstructing my mouth. My jaw opens, but hair doesn't fall in. I stretch my tongue out, capture some and bite. Chewing now, I break the weak hairs and keep chewing. I swallow, swallow, force my throat to hold against my gag reflex.

When Carson comes back to the car, I'm twisting my hair to one side to mask the missing chunk. A few stray strands still try climbing back up my throat and into my mouth. A sparrow trying to escape.

Almost on the road to British Columbia. I don't want to seem to be going back to anywhere. Not back home, not until I find Devin. I have to try Nelson. The drive via Roger's Pass is better, less risk of snowstorms, of rolling off the side of a mountain, but Devin never did anything easy. I opt for the Crowsnest, following Arachne's flight and hoping I won't come across moonshine and a man selling a mine. First, though, Carson asked me to stop in Medicine Hat. There's a friend he hasn't seen in a while, and something he's gotta pick up for another friend, "and anyway it's not that big of a detour." I bartered that he pays for gas until we get to Nelson. A couple extra hours can't hurt when Devin's been missing for years. Besides, I'll find her. I have to.

The sun shines low, right in my line of sight. Squinting, I dig for my sunglasses in my bag on the backseat. Carson moved it. Usually I leave it on the passenger seat. Usually I don't have passengers that can move my shit. Just stiffs that wear my sunglasses and hold my bag for me. Real gentlemen.

One hand on the steering wheel, one distracted eye on the road, I swerve into the oncoming lane. I correct, sit straight, both hands in the proper positions on the wheel. No one in the other lane.

"What do you need?"

"Sunglasses, they're right on top of everything in my bag."

Carson, heaves my purse onto his lap, unzips it and retrieves them.

"If you hadn't moved my bag in the first place, I'd have been just fine."

"Or you could say *thank you.*"

I grab my sunglasses and fit them over my eyes, not responding.

"What've you got in this anyway?" Carson bobs my purse like he's weightlifting. "Feels like you robbed someone and put the spoils in here."

"Leave my stuff alone."

"Why keep all this?" Carson lifts out a handful of receipts and two empty cigarette packs.

I breathe deeply through my nose, counting the exhales. One two three four five and I'm out of breath. In and hold and out and hold. Carson ignores my silence and tosses my bag at his feet, the zipper still undone. I'm glad he's paying for gas, but part of me longs for another corpse. Still. Silent.

The recently dead make for excellent companions—the living? Well, I'm not so sure.

Devin and I never had our own cars—we borrowed my dad's old Maxima when we wanted to go out. After we learned how to drive standard. I never learned, could never time releasing the clutch and shifting gears. Devin drove me around. I got an automatic, after she left. Tried to outrun her stories. The ones tethered to my room.

Devin, curled on our armchair, the one we hauled four blocks after finding it on the side of the road with a "free" sign taped to the back. Keeping her distance. Usually we sat on the chair together and shared funny stories and drank tea. After living with me for most of a year, she relented and began drinking black tea. Earl Grey, mostly, with just a splash of milk. The same way I take my mine.

But when Devin gets like this, I know to leave her, and she'll eventually talk. If I pester her, she gets quieter, more reserved, and won't come back out for days.

"One time I was at a bar and a bartender spiked my drink and I collapsed outside." She says it without pause and without rushing. No punctuation or inflection.

I'm at my dresser, looking in the mirror, arranging my face so I don't show concern, pity, sympathy. I continue experimenting with my new makeup. Dark silver and purple eyeliner, and wait.

"Out with friends, underage, but I had a fake that got me in. We sat at the bar and had the guy mix us whatever he wanted. His name was Collin. At least four shots and syrupy sweet, we called the drink *fuck me hard, Collin*, and ordered more by that name. He was in his twenties, had a five o'clock shadow, but it was after midnight."

Pull my bottom lid down to get the eyeliner just right along the rim.

"I was fine, and then I was not. Not okay. I don't know how I got to the washroom, I don't even remember being there, but my friends told me I went there of my own accord, and Collin came to get me when the bar was closed because he was concerned, and my friends were too drunk to care."

Still. Hands down, one eye finished with white sparkles over the tear ducts and under my eyebrow. Devin said highlighting will make my round eyes look bigger. Innocent. I will learn later to highlight with a sparkly beige, because white makes me look sickly.

"I only remember the sidewalk cold and hard against my skin, and rolling to support myself in recovery position, one arm under my head, the other in a triangle for support. Moving a leg across my body for another support point, and an open burning inside."

I don't know what to say, and this is a precursor to my inability to comfort people when a loved one dies. But it's different because Devin is here, in my room, and I know she's safe, even if she doesn't. How do I tell her? She won't accept a hug or tears or a stiff *I'm sorry*. Devin sips her tea as if she didn't say anything, as if she doesn't need comfort, and I raise my makeup brush to finish my other eye.

It's morning, and I drove all night. I can't continue. Too tired. At least I know now that I can fall asleep and wake, and I will remember that Devin waits for me, just ahead. I have yet to sleep and forget. To give up my search. We'll get to Nelson soon enough, find Devin soon enough. If it were just me, I'd find a back road and stay in my car, get some sleep, move on. But with Carson here, well, I don't know. I suggest finding a motel or inn or something.

"Pay someone else so we can sleep? That's what you want to do."

"Do you have a better idea?" I snap, more tired than angry.

Carson offered to drive an hour or so back, but I didn't respond, and he dropped the idea. The drive from Forestburg should have taken about six hours, but we started late and detoured through Medicine Hat, where Carson met his friend and traded his duffle bag for a backpack. He bought me dinner at the A&W, so I didn't complain, and I didn't ask for further details.

"We can camp. There's plenty of grounds around here."

"We don't have a tent." I don't move my eyes from the road, try not to blink. Once you get blinking or distracted, the road can take you.

"Not yet." And I can see his grin though I don't move a muscle.

I pull into a grocery store parking lot. A few RVs and cars, vans, but not a lot. It's too early for locals to be shopping. Too early in the season for casual campers. Carson says he has a friend he can get a tent from around here. He seems to have friends everywhere. While he tracks down a tent, I'm tasked with hunting for breakfast. I enter the bright store, relieved that it's open so early. Hopefully they'll have fresh sandwiches.

All grocery stores are the same, departments organized to funnel you through before you arrive at what you came for. I grab a case of bottled water and four overpriced sandwiches. Turkey and Havarti, beef and Swiss, ham and cheddar, egg salad. I don't know what Carson likes, so one of each. At least the tags show the sandwiches were made this morning. Outside, Carson leans against my car, grey tent bag at his feet, cigarette smoke trailing from his mouth.

"That was fast."

"I told you I knew what I was doing."

"Still, a friend who'll get up at what, seven am? To give you a tent. And in the middle of nowhere? That's luck." I arch my back, crack my spine, then settle against my car, our hips touching.

"Luck has nothing to do with it. And Fernie isn't nowhere, lots of people live here."

"Lots of people just willing to part with a tent?" Convenient.

"Let's get going."

We find a lake thirty kilometres or so out of Fernie. Actually, Carson directs me down a dirt road lined with nearly dead trees, and there's a surprisingly not-frozen lake back from the road. The morning sun shines on the still water, a steady stream of light, like it's searching for something. For why it rose today. Of course, the sun doesn't think, doesn't wonder. Carson sets up the tent. I'm thoroughly unhelpful. I haven't camped since I was little.

IN REVERSE

Dad, Mom, and I go one summer, Canada Day long weekend. We drive up to Tofino, four-and-a-half hours from Victoria. We share a tent pitched at a campsite practically on the beach. On grass that touches sand. Dad sets up the tent, gets the fire going. Mom and I are on the beach. She spreads out on a white towel, stomach down, reading one of her adult books with a man and woman on the cover, his hand on her face. I make a sandcastle, use the wet sand to sculpt and the fine, dry sand to cover my masterpiece. A couple other kids come over and join me, help dig a trench that becomes a moat complete with a sea monster provided by another kid.

That was before Devin. Dad and I never went camping after Mom left.

There's no beach around this lake, just stubbly grass, and rocks about the size of quarters or loonies. I take a sandwich—turkey and Havarti—and sit on the rocks, bare feet dipped in the cool water, pants rolled up my calves. Peel back the top slice of bread. Shredded lettuce sticks to the mayo. I sift through the ingredients: deli turkey, one slice of Havarti, as promised, and tomatoes, red onion. With my finger and thumb, I pick all the onion strands off and toss them behind me to the magpies and geese. Replace the bread and take a bite. Then another.

Carson's set up the tent by the time I finish breakfast. I relocate my car blanket and a bulky sweater to the tent. Bunch the sweater into a makeshift pillow. I'm asleep before Carson zips the flap closed.

When I wake, Carson's in the lake. The sun, low in the sky now, plays with the ripples from his long strokes. I have no idea if Carson slept too, but if he did, he came in after me and got up before.

"Come on in!" He calls when he notices I'm watching him.

"Aren't you cold? It's basically winter!"

"It's April. Definitely spring."

Unconvinced, I dig in my suitcase for my swimsuit anyway. It's a bit small. I bought it with Devin. Matching bikinis for our Europe trip. Mine was purple, hers black—she said dark colours look better in the water. But that was before my hips really came in, not that they're huge, but the bottoms pinch my sides now. At least there aren't many people out here, and if I get in the water quickly, Carson might not notice. And I won't have time to chicken out from the cold. I take a running start and plunge, the water splashing around my shoulders and into my eyes.

Standing, the lake lapping at my chest, I gasp for breath. The water is frigid, pressing in on my lungs. I'm pushing my hair away from my face and sucking in air like I almost drowned when Carson swims over. He looks at me, head tilted, extends both arms outward, and I know what he's doing a moment before. He brings his hands together, pushing the water into a tidal splash that crashes over me.

"Hey!" I shout, but he's already dashed away, legs kicking up water behind him.

I front crawl after him. He doesn't know I took swimming lessons every summer through high school. I catch up, propel myself over his back, place my hands on his shoulders, and shove him under. Then it's my turn to run. Carson reaches me faster than I thought he would, and maybe he was going purposely slow when I dunked him. We engage in a close-range splashing war, taking turns being doused and doing the dousing. Our movements keep me warm, prevent the cold from really burrowing in. My body remembers to breathe.

Laughing, I don't know who gives up first. We've drifted further into the lake, and I try to stand, but the water's deeper here, and my toes can't touch the bottom. Instinctively, I grab Carson to avoid falling under. He pulls me closer, and I feel a slight thump against my thigh. And again. Then I realize what it is. I blush, and swim back to shore. Carson doesn't follow until I've dried off and changed into yoga pants and a sweater. I shiver on shore and wait for him to come back.

He isn't wearing swim trunks, isn't wearing anything. Water streams over his skin. Between his legs, Carson's cock hangs limp, water dripping. Drip. Drip. Clear, and nothing like the blood over Devin's teeth after our water fight.

We spent the night by the lake—no sense in driving late again and wasting the next day. Today we'll get to Nelson. Today I'll be closer to finding Devin.

Carson slept next to me last night, didn't try to touch me, but I'm curious.

As I drive, I place my right hand on his knee. He shifts, moves his leg out, closer to me, and I bring my hand further up his thigh. We're listening to the CD Devin made me, and I tap my fingers with the beat. I think I'm moving them slowly up and up, but too soon I touch his zipper. Carson squirms just a little. I glance at him, raise my eyebrows.

"Pigeon."

I don't answer. I forget my name for a moment.

"Pigeon," he says again, and undoes the button on his jeans.

My hand is still, resting on his crotch. I feel his cock thump again. He lowers the zipper, and I press down, feel him through his boxers.

"Pigeon."

"I'm not Pigeon," I answer as he shuffles his jeans and boxers down, freeing his dick. It waves at me from the corner of my eye, my focus directed at the road.

"Then who are you?"

In response, I grab his cock, my middle and index fingers wrap around to meet my thumb and slowly, slowly I pull them up his shaft. I rub small circles with my thumb at the top, over his tip, and he shudders, a small amount of fluid oozes out. I coat my fingers in his discharge and drag them down, then up. Again and again, and slowly, faster and faster. Carson's hips move to help me, my angle awkward over the console.

My breathing becomes shallow, uneven. I take my left hand off the wheel, reach under my skirts, and feel the damp between my legs. I've never been turned on by a man before. Maybe I'm just impressed with myself—with how much he wants me.

Hand back on the steering wheel, I smile, just a little.

"Isn't road head the other way around?"

"I'm not using my mouth."

I continue to move my hand, quickly now. He spits into his own hand and interrupts my rhythm to spread his saliva as a lube. Trees drop beside me, the mountain curving downward.

"Pigeon."

"I'm not Pigeon."

"Pigeon. I'm going . . . going . . . to cum."

I smile wide, feel that my face must look demented, teeth piercing my lower lip, cheeks raised, making my eyes squint. Hopefully he's too distracted to notice me.

"Cum on my legs."

"What?"

"Cum on my legs."

Carson unbuckles his seatbelt, takes my hand off his dick and pumps himself. His frame blocking my view. Warm, almost clear, milky semen squirts onto my right thigh. I rub it into my skin. Slick against my palm, between my fingers. Without thinking, I touch my cunt, still wet, then bring my fingers to my lips. Taste us. Carson's already pulled out my towel from the backseat, unpacked from our swim, and cleans himself.

"That was something new for me." He slumps back into the seat.

"Was it good?" I take my eyes off the road for the first time to really look at him.

A loud thunk. My front wheel jolts. Skids, and the car spins out of the lane. I yank the steering wheel in the opposite direction, away from the edge of the cliff face, the drop. The car straightens, and I pull over. Every muscle in my body so tense I worry I'll stomp through the brake pedal. We lurch to a stop. My fingers not quite able to grip the emergency break, still slick, slip off the handle as I try to engage the lock. Shaking, I put on the hazard lights and get out. My legs collapse under me and my knee hits the pavement hard. None of the wheels seem damaged, popped. From my kneeling position, I can see a dark liquid leaking from under my car. Fuck. I swivel on the ground to get a better look. Carson hasn't moved.

Fuck him.

He didn't clean off my thigh. Grit from the road leeches to his leftover sheen. My scraped knee bleeds into the cement.

"Pigeon?"

Staring at the underside of my car, the metal and plastic and whatever else, I spit out: "I'm not Pigeon, goddamnit, how many times do I have to tell you?"

"What did you hit?"

"What did I hit? You had nothing to do with this? You and your goddamned cock."

"Woah. Calm down." Beside me now, Carson puts his hand on my shoulder.

"Don't touch me! Don't fucking touch me."

He backs away, crouches at the front of my car. Shines his cellphone flashlight underneath. "Looks like it's either the transmission or the cooling tube for the transmission."

Back against the tire, arms crossed.

"If it's the tube, we're in good shape. Little bit of electricians' tape for now, find a replacement at any hardware store."

The reddish liquid seeps beside me, trickles under my ass. I stand, try to wring out my skirt.

"But if it's the transmission, you're fucked."

"Last time I looked, you're stuck too."

"Not my car. If I'd been driving, we would still be headed toward Nelson."

"Fine, you can stay here."

I get back into my car. Turn the key, but the engine won't roll over. Jiggle the gearshift. Stuck. Try to take my keys but the ignition holds them. "Fucking hell." Step out of the car, slam the door.

"What, can't leave me behind, honey?"

I fish my phone from my purse. No signal. I hold it up, walk around the bend in the road. Still nothing. Go back to my car, sit in the drivers' seat, leave the door open to diffuse some of the heat and light a cigarette. Shouldn't there be snow in the mountains this time of year? Not fucking sunshine and potholes?

"Aren't you good at problem solving."

"You've got a better idea?"

He doesn't. Pulls out his own cigarette and smokes, sitting on the trunk of my car.

The sun arcs over us, the mountains acting as a funnel for the heat. I try to turn my key partially, just enough for the air conditioning to come on, but now it's so stuck it won't move at all. Carson's face and neck glow pink, a sweat stain marks his spine. I remove my bra, knot my shirt above my navel, kick my shoes off and into the middle of the road.

No one drives past.

"Aren't you hot?" I break the silence, but the thick air muffles my voice.

He doesn't answer.

"I'm going for a walk." I declare.

The gravel on the highway pricks my soles. I won't turn back for my shoes. Light another cigarette and throw my shoulders back, because what's the use of crying or screaming or sitting in my car?

I round the bend. Twenty minutes of walking, and I can't see my car, but I can see the road better. Nothing, no one.

And then a shimmer followed by a puff of dust. Blink, still there. A rumble with a hidden whine grows louder as the car approaches. I wave both arms, erratic, frantic. I can't stay stuck with Carson for much longer.

The dusty blue sedan pulls over. A man with arms that look permanently tanned rolls down his window. "What's the problem?"

"My car. Must've hit something, and now it won't go. Just around the corner."

"Hop in and we'll see what we can do."

"Thanks."

I relax against the carpeted seat. Air conditioning already on full blast. But it's only a one-minute drive, and he gets out, so I have to get out, and Carson barely looks surprised. More like he expected me to find someone, and I accomplished the task faster than anticipated.

"Hey, man, what've you guys got yourselves into?" The dusty man shakes Carson's hand.

The two of them bend to examine the pool of car blood.

"Well, something got smashed real good." The dusty man addresses Carson.

"The front tire hit something, and there was a clunk, and the gear shift and ignition are all gummed up." I crouch beside them. It's my goddamn car.

"That would be the potholes or rocks back there, I would guess. Likely a rock that bounced under a few times. Mountain roads."

The man flattens his stomach on the ground, getting a better look at the still growing stain. Maybe my car just had the orgasm of its life, and now it's done.

"Looks like the transmission."

"Damn."

"Need a ride into town? We're about twenty clicks out of Nelson. Five mins or so. You can get a friend or a tow, seeing as how reception isn't much good out here."

"Yeah, yeah. We can do that." I look over at Carson. He has friends everywhere. And he works with cars.

"Thanks, man." Carson shakes the dusty man's hand, as if the two of them are in charge and I'm an inconsequential annoyance. A little sister tagging along.

From the visor, I grab my bulldog clip with the two photos. An effort to take Devin with me. And my purse, overflowing with the detritus Carson labelled as junk, and my book. Leave my blanket, my suitcase with assorted clothes in my car, like I left my kettle and laptop and mattress in my apartment.

Just like that, I leave my car on a mountain side, keys stuck in the ignition. Four years and ninety-two thousand kilometres we travelled together. I walk away, sit in the dusty man's comfortable Camry.

My eyes sting, so I look up and blink, blink.

IN REVERSE

I got my car after Devin. After they told me she died. Couldn't stay in the house, where I still heard her footsteps across the kitchen. Saw her reflection in mirrors. Heard her voice whisper through the clink of a spoon stirring milk into tea.

I needed a car so I could flee from her stories. My room wasn't the safe place where we shared secrets. It had become an archive for every reason and action that led Devin to me—our stories pinned to walls like dead butterflies to boards, framed. And because of me, she died.

I drove fast. Out of the city, to the docks in Sidney, to every beach I knew. Once even to Tofino, just to realize that the entire island held her worst secrets. Caged her darkness in the roiling waves while everything good seemed to evaporate. Her voice, telling and retelling her stories, intertwined with the salt breeze. I used my car to run away from her calls for help, and now I'm driving to find her. Searching. Overturning places and experiences, hoping she's hiding somewhere. The ocean of prairies didn't speak.

I've been in reverse since she left. Died. Fled. Escaped. Devin found freedom, one way or another, and I'm stuck. Between two realities. My memories lapse, loop, my imagination fills in the gaps, and I try to be honest, really, but I can't tell the difference, not all the time. And what does it matter, truth, when a good story's involved? Devin told me that. Or I told her.

She never drove through the mountains, but I imagine she would have liked to. Would have pressed herself between the crevasses and fissures in the rock faces. Would have loved the beauty, touched her hands to the mountains and willed her fingerprints to stay. But she would not have stayed here, too contained, like the Island. The mountains just another version of ocean, and I have to keep going. She left all her stories behind.

I try not to think of all her new stories. The ones that don't include me.

"I'm gonna keep calling you Pigeon," Carson declares around his double-patty cheeseburger.

The dusty man dropped us off on a main road. Even his dashboard and car seats were dusty. We walked and found another A&W—Carson's favourite fast food stop, apparently—and then we kept walking.

"Fine by me." I munch my burger. Look at the water as we stop on the far end of a dock. "What are we doing with my car?"

"I've got a friend who can lend us a car if you want to keep going. Yours is a write-off, with the transmission smashed."

"I can't just leave my car on the side of the road."

He shrugs. "I'll get someone to pick it up."

Fuck Carson. All his solutions.

A small shop tucked off the main street catches my eye. Bright tie-dyed banner unfurled above the door with a black symbol—ohm—and crystals in the window. I point it out to Carson—he says he doesn't have time, needs to find us a new ride. We've been here over a week already. Another friend of his lent us a tent, and we've been camping outside the town. Hiking in every morning, going our separate ways for most of the day. I search for Devin in alleyways and bars. No idea what Carson does during the day—don't know why he stays, either. Maybe he's lonely or bored, or has nowhere else to be, or is stocking up on supplies or drugs or whatever else he's peddling, because I'm fairly sure he doesn't work with cars. But, to his credit, he hasn't brought up our brief sexual encounter and subsequent car crash. He calls me Pigeon, and I believe he has generous friends scattered across Alberta and the Rockies.

I enter the dim store alone. Keelie and Clive and Pigeon would go to this store. Devin might. The counter faces the door and stretches to the far corners. One side has small bins of gems, paper slips indicating their names and properties. Hematite for grounding, jade for good luck, kyanite for spiritual communications. I pick through a few. Settle on rose quartz.

At the counter, a white girl with long dreads helps a couple find a book on tarot.

I place my chosen stone on the counter after the couple leaves. "Hi, just this."

"The love stone. Must be a gift for someone special." She touches the stone pendant on her necklace, wire wrapped rose quartz on a twine string.

"Yeah, I'm actually looking for her, mind if I show you a picture?"

"Yeah, no worries. That comes to four dollars and twenty-three cents, with tax."

I pass her a five. "Do you recognize her?" I take out my picture of Devin, the one where she's hiding her smile with a fork. Don't bother with the internet picture—I'm tired of people coming up with stories, excuses, false explanations. They're just distractions.

"Hmm, no. Never seen her. Does she live around here?"

"Just visiting." I take my stone, rubbing its face, the rough surface on my thumb. I don't thank her, don't take my change. Leave.

Outside, Carson's in the driver's seat of a giant SUV. Clean, silver, dark leather interior reeking of money, that warm smell of perfumed animal hide.

"You've got a nice friend."

Couldn't he have borrowed a less conspicuous car?

Nelson was a bust. Carson's at the wheel, I doze, not sure exactly where we are or where he's heading. I'm getting further and further away from Devin. Grasping at any hint and driving, just driving anywhere she might be. Could be. But isn't.

Behind us, a sporty car revs, moves to pass, but Carson speeds up in response. Sirens interrupt our CD, a mix Carson's friend left in the car. The friend must have a family, because the tracks alternate between Bon Jovi, Taylor Swift, and some sort of heavy metal.

I didn't save my CD from my car. Devin's mix trapped in a dead stereo.

Blue and red lights issue from the car behind us, reflecting off the side mirrors. Carson pulls over, cursing under his breath. Didn't expect to see a ghost car all the way out here.

"Do you know the speed limit here?" The officer leans over Carson's open window, his sunglasses showing Carson his own face.

Innocent smile. "Hundred and ten, isn't it?" I almost believe him.

"No, ninety on this road. Sign posted just back there," the officer gestures with a thumb to the back of the white sign, still easily visible.

"Ah."

"You were doing one-twenty, boy. I need to see your licence, registration, and insurance."

Carson pulls his wallet from his back pocket awkwardly and passes his licence over.

I make a show of waking up, yawning, and stretching. "We borrowed this car, so it might take a little to find the other stuff," I pitch in, hoping to save myself, before opening the glove box to search. I keep my papers in the glove box.

"I see. Well how about you guys look, and I'll run your plates in case you can't find it." He walks back to his ghost car, not a swagger or meander. Just a nice, normal guy walk. Good, hopefully he'll let us off easy.

"Why the hell would you tell him that?" Carson hisses at me, brow furrowed and lips tight.

"Well, what if we can't find the registration or insurance? It's not in here, and we could get ticketed for not having proof." And because you're a fucking show-off.

"This is on you."

The officer comes back, standing a bit straighter than before. "Can you please step out of the car, hands up."

"What? Why?" I jump out, but he's talking to Carson.

"This car was reported as stolen, I need you both to come with me."

"He's a rich snob. Two SUVs, a Porsche, and a Tesla Model S. I'm surprised he even noticed this one was missing." Carson spits on his recently vacated seat through the open window.

"Yes, and you're a regular Robin Hood."

Carson's in a holding cell, while I get a waiting-room chair. The officer vouched for me. Said I had no idea what Carson did. Which I didn't. The cop, a sympathetic half smile on his face, "Don't you have someone to call, come pick you up? Your mom or dad?"

My dad, with his grilled cheese sandwiches and filing cabinet of memories and normal girlfriend who has never asked me to call her mom. No, I can't call him. I don't want this failure locked in a drawer with my others. My mom, who couldn't deal with me years ago, couldn't deal with this either. I don't even know her number. But Devin's dad, my uncle. It's worth a try.

Hey, Uncle Roy. I'm in a bit of trouble. No, no, I'm fine, but I'm in jail. No, I didn't do anything this time. No, Dad doesn't know. I just, I'm wondering if you could come pick me up? I know you're pretty far away, but so is everyone else.

Lines rehearsed, it's worth a try.

Uncle Roy, Dad's brother, squats on the stairs to our front porch. We were both adopted. Him by parents who couldn't conceive until they adopted him and then realized my dad was already on the way, and me by the stepmother who later decided she didn't want me.

When I first met Roy, I was a child, newly claimed and yet to be cast aside, and I felt he was true family. Both of us bound because we were special enough to be wanted. After Mom left, he didn't treat me any differently. Didn't pity me or offer those flaccid condolences, the "it's not you, it's her choice to leave," that his wife, my aunt Jocelyn, gave, even when everyone knew it was entirely because of me.

He just got in from Calgary. I liked him better last time he visited, when Devin came to live here. But maybe he only laughed and joked because he was glad to be rid of her. No. No one is happy when Devin leaves.

I walk past him, gesture something indiscernible. Something like *I'm sorry*.

And I want to tease him about his dad-shirt, the plaid button-up tucked into his jeans, like I did last time I saw him. I want to act normal and treat him like he treated me. But my mom didn't die, she just decided to not be my mom. A smaller death.

"You go ahead. Roy and I are going to sit out here for a bit." My dad drinks some of the amber liquid from his glass. Whiskey brought out only for special occasions, Christmas dinner, a milestone birthday, or, like today, the day before a funeral.

I didn't say goodbye to Carson. We didn't know each other, so I don't know what the etiquette is. A car thief. A tent thief. Does he have any friends?

My aunt, next to me, driving, hair cut in an angular bob, trailing from the nape of her neck along her jawline. It's shorter than last time I saw her. More severe.

My uncle stayed home with Dacy. Couldn't come, or didn't want to?

I watch my aunt's neck and shoulder muscles contract and relax, over and over. She doesn't believe I had nothing to do with the car. She wants to, but she doesn't. What did I expect? She sent Devin to live with me for a reason.

Devin, with friends like Clive and Keelie and Pigeon, and the girl with the flower in her hair, and all the people with dreads, talking about communism and the way everything comes back around. Cyclical. Young people, educated, not as educated as they think, and living on the outskirts of reality. Living as artists. No real jobs, just making money to pay for a room, food, alcohol, and drugs. If it had just been pot, weed, marijuana, they—my aunt—could've dealt with her. But a small pack of white powder and thin strips, hidden in separate plastic bags in her top drawer next to a string of condoms and a pink vibrator. The next morning, Devin was shipped away. Given to me, because "Calgary isn't good for her." The city blamed as a bad influence.

Living in Victoria, what was my excuse?

Our parents agreed we might be able to help each other. Besides, Mom had already left. I was a graduate of the rehab program—reformed as a model teenager. My dad said I needed someone, another girl. That giving Devin the responsibility of being a good role model for me would help her more than any punishment. I listened in on the phone calls from the house phone in the kitchen when Dad called Aunt Jocelyn from the phone in his bedroom. Made sure to breathe very quietly so no one would know I was listening. I was excited. Ecstatic. I'd only seen Devin when we were children, but even back then she'd had the best ideas. The pinnacle was pranking our parents with rubber rats in unsuspecting places—the fridge, under gas pedals, inside coat pockets. I kept up the shenanigans after she left, went back home, but it wasn't the same.

My aunt hasn't asked me what I was doing in the middle of BC, driving around with a stranger. Where my car is. Why I didn't call my dad.

Her neck muscles pulse, and she doesn't say a word for the first three hours of our drive. Not until we get to Golden, and she asks if I need the washroom while she tops up the gas. After that, another stretch of silence. Maybe she's afraid to know what I was doing. Maybe she fights to keep her tongue under wraps to save herself from knowing. If I don't explain, then she can imagine anything, can keep all the blame squarely on me.

It felt like my mom left us while Dad drove me home from the police station. As I remember it, we got home, and she was gone. Only ten minutes, but it was the longest drive of my life.

But that's not right. She stayed, for a while. She took the picture of my dad and me in our matching Christmas sweaters a month after my *incident*, as she referred to it. Mom had a matching sweater too. Red and white stripes with green reindeer. Knitted. She bought them from a local knitter—a work friend's sister or something. Trying to make us look like one of those picture-perfect families. All we needed was a golden retriever and a white fence.

But as much as she tried, she wasn't really there. She gave up on me. Gave me up as easily as she took me in. I wasn't really hers. And I knew that before she left. But I wanted her to prove me wrong. I wanted to push and push her away, and for her to hold tighter and stay with me, to prove that she really did want me. Would always choose me.

I tell this to Devin. One night, when I can't sleep. I crawl into bed with her, under the covers. On my back, staring at the dark ceiling, not even looking at her. I tell Devin, even though she's only been here two months and we still don't really know each other, but I miss when we shared my room, at the beginning. She listens. Her breathing calm, real slow, and even.

I think she's fallen asleep, her breathing so shallow. Until she speaks, tells me about how her mom named her. *Devon* chosen for the son Jocelyn wanted. "I've always thought the difference between the *o* and the *i* in the spelling of my name is how my mom thinks about boys and girls, men and women. One is allowed to take up space, and the other has to get as slim as possible. Not in a physical sense, but more like attention. Like guys can be monuments, admired, and girls, well, we're only good as casual wall art. Flat, decorative." I don't say anything, and Devin continues, "Just. Ugh, it's hard to explain. But I feel like no matter what I do, it doesn't matter. My mom doesn't want me to do or experience things. She'd rather I passively coast through school, follow her trajectory, get a husband, some kids, maybe a fucking dog."

I don't respond. Pretend I am asleep. I want Devin to comfort me, not the other way around. Want to talk about my mother issues, not hers.

Rant done, she rolls over and hugs me, and we fall asleep like that. Her arm across my chest.

DRIVING

Maybe she doesn't understand.

I start talking about how I crashed. Told her I hit a rock that rolled down from the mountain. Left my car just outside of Nelson. That I didn't call insurance, but maybe I should. That a dusty man said the transmission was broken, and I didn't think. I panicked.

She doesn't say anything. The whole seven-hour drive, back through the mountains. Revelstoke and Roger's Pass, and gas in Golden. Back through Banff and Canmore. Doesn't stop driving.

We get to her house late. Not too late, but it's dark. Pull into the garage. We sit in silence, still, until she speaks.

"You'll be staying in the guest room. Dacy doesn't mind lending you clothes until your dad sends yours out, or you buy some. You didn't bring a suitcase."

I forgot everything in my car. "You talked to Dad?" Everything except my purse, my photos, book.

"He has a right to know where his daughter is."

"I'll leave as soon as I can." I blow out air from my cheeks. An intimation of blowing smoke. Haven't had a cigarette in almost a day, not since being pulled over, so many kilometres ago. My head feels fuzzy, clouded.

"Are you going home?"

"No." I look at her profile again, except that she's already turned to look at me, and neither of us has moved to get out of the car.

"Then you're staying here for a while. Until you're better."

I want to argue that there's nothing wrong with me. I'm fine, I'm fine. But the look on her face, the stubborn set of her chin, soft lines on her forehead and around her lips. It's like I'm seeing a future version of Devin, and I know she wants to take care of me.

"Thanks." My shoulders relax.

Didn't realize I'd been tensed until now. The offer of a safe place, warm, steady, stable. I won't give up looking for Devin, but I can rest and re-evaluate where to go next. Make a plan. Follow through. That's what the group therapy sessions advised, when things get too hard.

We unbuckle ourselves, then head into the house, the garage leading first into a laundry room, three piles of clothes in front of the washing machine. Whites, darks, pinks. The same way Dad organizes his laundry, though his pink pile is red. My aunt guides me to the living room, I sit on the leather couch, because that seems to be what she wants. My uncle's watching TV, a comedy show, he pats my knee like I'm the same little girl he found flinging miniature berries from their tree into their neighbour's back yard the time Dad took me to visit my cousins. Like I wasn't really in trouble, but I'd still done something wrong. Like a light scolding would solve all my problems.

I smile at him. "Hi." Chew on my hangnail and bundle my knees up into my stomach.

Uncle Roy turns down the volume. "How're you doing?"

"Fine, not my first jail cell." I smile again.

"As long as it doesn't become a habit. You're not a kid anymore, they won't let you off so easy as before."

"Because the psych ward was easy." I roll my eyes, but know he means well, and it's not like I spent much time in the hospital anyway.

"Would anyone like tea?" Dacy skips down the stairs wearing a baggy sweater hanging off her shoulder and ripped skinny jeans.

She must be in high school now. Must be fashion conscious, even at home. But that's not what I see when she's standing in front of the couch asking about tea, and my aunt replies yes for everyone.

My old living room, my dad's living room. Cloth couches. One normal sized, the other a loveseat, mismatched. Flowers and stripes. Mom took the leather couches when she left—she knew Dad had these in storage. His mom's, my grandma's, ugly, but he couldn't part with them after she died.

My aunt and Uncle Roy on the loveseat, Jocelyn crying, a blanket around her shoulders, held by my uncle's secure fingers. My dad standing unsure behind me on the couch. My arms around my knees at my chin. And Dacy. Standing a little away, tears streaking her face, but not smudging her makeup, because she didn't wear any back then. Dacy, so small and unsure, only twelve years old, asking if anyone wanted tea. She was the intruder. In my house, offering me my tea.

But I was the intruder. Because Devin was her sister, and I was the one incapacitated with her parents. Claw marks down my face, trying to gouge away my own tears, but they kept pouring over the raised red marks. Black mascara under my nails.

I take my mug of tea. Orange Pekoe, no milk or sugar.

"Thanks," I lift my mug at her, nearly spilling she's filled it so high.

Dacy sits next to me after handing out mugs to everyone. "It's been a while."

"Since the funeral," I say, automatically, and realize I should've said four and a half years. But it's all the same, so maybe it doesn't matter.

A laugh track from the comedy show plays, and Uncle Roy turns the TV off. Dacy stares into her mug. The silence is worse than the background of jokes.

I can't help myself. "You look like Devin. Same face."

"Yeah."

My aunt and uncle sit stiff on either side of us, fingers tight on their mugs, not drinking. Dacy's given us all matching mugs, white outside, purple inside, wide mouths.

"You're in high school now?"

"Grade 11." Dacy sits straight, lifts her chin. Proud. "I just turned seventeen."

I'd just turned seventeen before going to England and Paris with Devin. She was still eighteen, about to turn nineteen in the fall, but she never got to. Devin died with under a month until she could legally drink in BC. I don't know how, but I graduated high school the following June, when I turned eighteen. Dad said I could take my time—recover. Process my grief. Graduate a year late. But I refused. Ripped up our photos, memories, and forgot about Devin.

I sip my tea, nodding. Uncle Roy stands, mutters that we need a snack with the tea. Puts down his mug and goes to the kitchen. I become aware of the stretching silence. I'm not good at small talk, at least not with family. I've only been talking to strangers lately.

I clear my throat. "Wow. Wow. That's awesome. You've grown a lot. Happy birthday"

Dacy doesn't seem to mind the long gaps between my responses, shoots back an immediate, "Thanks. I hear you're in university," as if she'd been waiting to say that, her words preplanned.

"What do you want to do when you graduate?"

"I don't know. Maybe I'll be a doctor, make people better. Help people." She blows on her tea.

Uncle Roy returns with a plate of biscuits. The kind with chocolate bottoms. He sets the plate on the coffee table in front of us. My aunt, stiff beside Dacy, doesn't respond except to rotate the mug in her hands.

"That's a good goal." I smile at Dacy.

We each reach for a biscuit. My aunt takes her first sip of tea. An inaudible group sigh.

The spare room is bland. Pale green walls and sheets. A white comforter with vines, their embroidered leaves unfurled. Framed pictures above the bed, the generic kind featuring a landscape with a small white flag, indicating a golf course, and blue sky. The only real colour a vase, half full of clear marbles and a single shoot of bamboo. At least it's alive.

I walk down the hall to the bathroom. The room's theme is blue beaches. At least, that's what I gather from the aqua walls and shell shaped soap dish. An obviously handmade incense holder rests on the back of the toilet—a glass rectangle, sand-filled, shells and glitter stuck to the outside, with a half-burned stick wedged in at an angle. Despite these details, the room doesn't look as neglected as the guest room. It hasn't been done up like a mannequin and left behind a closed door. The bottles on the counter—face creams and perfumes—are scattered from use, the towel beside the shower hangs crooked, and spit stains trail toward the drain in the sink. A clean towel, facecloth, and still-wrapped toothbrush are stacked neatly on the toilet seat, I assume for me.

In the mirror I watch myself. I bring my hand up to the shaved side of my head, feel the soft stubble. The missing chunk on the other side of my hair makes my head look lopsided, or like a cat with a bad haircut because it kept flailing while being groomed. My eyes are ringed in dark circles. Large, red spots cover my chin and nose, I could feel the pimples forming, but I didn't realize they were this bad. I try to pop one, but my nails are jagged and catch on my skin. Tear a hole, small, and blood spurts out. My teeth have forgotten food caught between them and my eyebrows have grown almost together. And this is how my family found me. Unkempt, mangy, smelling like stale sweat and cigarettes, my clothes rumpled, stained. How long since I last showered? Camping with Carson, I barely noticed what I wore, smelled like. No wonder no one in Nelson had heard of Devin—they must've all been trying to get me to leave as fast as possible.

I shower, let the hot water berate me like my family should have. Pound into my skin, head. And then I make use of all the shampoos and body soaps lining the edge of the bathtub. Even carve into the bar of soap just to clean under my nails. I step out, wrap myself in the thick beige towel. Beige to match the colour of sand, presumably. Leave my clothes on top of the garbage next to the toilet.

Dacy's sitting cross-legged on my bed when I enter the guest room, folded fabric on her lap.

"I have clothes for you. PJs and other stuff. It's all clean."

"Thanks." I take the offered pants, pink and blue paisley on a white background, and the blue tank top. She took care to bring me a matching set.

"This used to be Devin's room," she supplies, detached, finger tracing a vine on the bedspread. "Mom redecorated after. After the funeral. Filled and sanded over the holes from her posters and pictures. Painted. Bought everything new."

Dad did the same. When Mom left, Dad kept her "meditation" room until Devin came. The second bedroom, a former guest room, Mom turned it into her space after my almost-arrest. She went up there to do yoga, listen to soft music that "captured the sounds of nature" and put her "more in tune with the universe." That's what she said. That she needed to be "retuned, balanced, harmonized." She hung long sheets of satin from the walls, bought metal bowls with mallets that sung when rapped on the side. A miniature fountain decorated with fairies, that never had water because she didn't want to ruin the carpet.

Dad believed it was her sacred space, that he couldn't disturb the it. That maybe, if he left the room intact, she might return, because it was her place to escape to, not from.

She went up there to smoke pot when I was being "difficult." Lit incense to cover the smell. I stole from her stash, because it mellowed me out. Made me easier for her to deal with. At least, that's what I thought.

I never told Dad.

A month into Devin living with me, sharing my room, dresser, bed, and side table, Dad tore down the first piece of fabric. We offered to help, but he said he had it under control. "Don't worry, I'll put you two to work later, bringing up the mattress."

Once the first panel was down, he kept tearing. Ripped pins from the walls and left holes and scratches in the paint. Dad threw out everything except the fountain. Put it in the garden and hooked it up so spluttering water cycled through all year, until the air got too cold and turned it to ice. Once, I told him to shut it off and empty it in winter, to help it last, but he said that "wasn't worth the effort."

We helped patch and paint the walls. Devin wanted tangerine, bright and obnoxious as a tiger lily. The colour we got was called "apricots and cream," almost neutral, but still tinged orange. The window opened to the east, and at sunrise Devin got shafts of her tangerine.

The guest room at my dad's is still the same. It was never really Devin's room.

"Do you miss her? Devin?" But the question sounds hollow and I want to ask about the mugs, pyjamas.

"She used to let me stay up past my bedtime if I painted her toenails for her. I pretended I hated it, said *feet are gross*, but I liked it. I liked doing something for her that made her happy. And I liked staying up late watching TV with her."

"I'm sorry." For what? That I took Devin? That Dacy always makes the tea?

"Me too." For reminding me that I have no claim to Devin? Or because she knows it's all my fault Devin had a funeral?

IN REVERSE

"I'm sorry," everyone says, "so sorry." They stop by with casseroles or homemade soups. Apologize.

"So young."

"So bright."

Just words. "Terrible," "tragic," "sorrow," "incomprehensible."

All words falling from mouths like drool. Because that's what you say when someone dies.

"I'm sorry."

In bed. In—most likely, probably—Devin's bed, curled on my side facing the window, dragging my eyes up and down the folds of the curtains, waiting for sleep. I should sleep, I should be exhausted, and maybe I am. But in Devin's bed, all I can remember is Devin in the hospital, and the way she curled toward the window at night. And I wonder if she was thinking of this view. Of the tree illuminated by the orange streetlamp, branches like paths she could have taken, could have taken to avoid ending up sick. But I don't think she did. I don't think she spent her nights wondering where else she could have been. She spent her nights planning her escape. Where she would go.

The bamboo on the side table catches my attention again, one stick, one path, an upward spiral. Reaching.

A small creak from the hallway and a broadening light over my shoulder, grasping for the bamboo. A shadow interrupts the light, solid, sits on the edge of my—Devin's—bed.

"You miss her too. Devin. You said her name earlier. Mom and Dad don't say her name anymore. They just call her my sister, like she isn't part of them."

"Everyone grieves differently." Hollow. Another piece of advice from therapy.

"How do you?" Dacy's voice, so tiny and young, like she's twelve again.

"I've been searching for her."

"But she's dead." Resolute, repeating aloud what she's had to remind herself every morning. Or at least that's how it was for me. Until I found the picture declaring otherwise.

The back deck is raised. A small square outlined by a waist-high railing. Wood. Splintering and spider infested, even though spring's barely begun. Webs grow from the railing to the barbeque, patio chairs, and table. I put my middle finger to a spider, his orange body bigger than my nail. I thought Calgary didn't have big spiders. That's what Devin told me.

Victoria does. Even bigger than these, long legs stretching over webs, claiming their domains. Wolf spiders, flat-bellied ground spiders, red orb weaver spiders. I suspect the orange spider here is a type of orb weaver, but neither it nor the small striped jumping spiders bother me, so I settle into a patio chair and ignore them.

"Coffee?" Dacy hands me a mug before sitting in the other chair.

I hold it in both hands. The same mug as last night, part of a set. Black coffee inside, except that coffee isn't ever a true black. But it could be, tinted dark by this mug.

"It's Devin's favourite blend." Dacy takes a long sip. "Mine too."

"New Orleans." It warms my fingers, protecting against the morning chill.

We sit and sip our coffee. Watch a spider repair its home. Look at the snow about to melt on the grass below us. Patches of green interrupt the white. We don't talk about Devin or redecorated rooms or anything else. I drink all the coffee, because it was Devin's favourite. Dark and acidic and bitter. "Deep flavour profile" pops into my mind. Regardless, I think I'll try making it weaker, like the barista at The Roasterie suggested. Watered down so it tastes like a tea. Maybe that's why Devin hasn't come to get me—she's complex, like this coffee, and she thinks I don't appreciate her right. Or maybe that I'm weak in comparison. I shake my head and feel a vibration from my chest. Caffeine. I'm not used to all this caffeine people keep giving me. My head can't handle it, and it makes me think funny. I try to remember if caffeine is linked to paranoia and decide it must be. That's why I keep thinking Devin is purposefully avoiding me.

No, that's not the paranoid thought. Believing that Devin is alive at all—that's the real craziness. How can I be here, with her family, and still believe that Devin is hiding? No matter that her parents shipped her off to be with me—she couldn't put her sister through this much pain.

Dacy takes our mugs to the dishwasher before going to school. I think about offering to drive her, then remember I don't have a car. My car is broken on a mountain road. Maybe I should call insurance. She leaves, and it's like I was always alone.

I stay outside. The sun hits the deck first, over the railing, onto my shoulder. No more cars leave. Children are at school, parents at work. Where they should be. And me. Here. I need a smoke.

Sun and silence and square fences surround me. The spider's finished her maintenance and crawled into a crevice, hiding. I can't go inside, the walls and furniture, paintings of nothing, and the wood dining set. At least out here there's a breeze. And a tabby strutting along the fence tops. From one end to the other, between boundaries.

Holding the railing, I peer at the fence, the gap's maybe two feet wide. I swing my left leg over the rail, then my right. My feet can touch the fence from where I'm sitting. Hands planted beside my hips, I try to push my weight to my feet. Arms strain, and a sharp stab in my finger must be a sliver. I reconsider, plant one foot on the fence and one on the deck railing, straddle the gap. I jolt the rest of my body onto the fence. Keep my arms ready to windmill. My bare toes curl over the edge. One step. Then another and another, and I don't have to look at my feet anymore.

From this vantage I can see all the yards. Gardens not yet tended, muddy splotches and slushy snow, a trampoline and toys strewn around. Any yard could be interchanged with any other. Except the one directly behind my aunt's house. A couch rests on four concrete slabs meant to be a deck, and grass doesn't show, even though most of the snow has melted. Weeds and the dead hard stalks of weeds cover the yard, tall and prickly.

The tabby saunters to me, rubs its face on my ankle. I try to kneel to scratch its ears. But I'm on a fence. My foot slips, pulls me off balance, over the edge. Shoulder hits the wet, over-grown weeds first. The tabby tilts its head down at me, meows.

Her tags jingle against each other, and she hops off the fence beside me. Meows in my face. Tabitha on her name tag. Tabitha the tabby standing at my ear, I reach to scratch her neck. Pain in my finger. I sit up, search for the sliver. A miniscule dot between the ridges of my fingerprint.

"Morning!" A woman in a blue robe, hair tied up, waves from the sofa. She wasn't there a moment ago, must've come outside when I fell.

Tabitha weaves through the weeds, curls on the woman's toes.

"I haven't seen you around," she continues.

"I don't live here," I mutter.

"Visiting?"

"Something like that." I stand, dirt sticking to my knees, and walk to the edge of the cement blocks, avoiding the pointiest weeds.

"I'm Thea. You don't have to fall off a fence if you want a chat." She stubs her cigarette, ashtray overflowing on the sofa arm.

"Thea. French?"

"Greek. My German-Ukrainian-Irish parents honeymooned in Greece. Nine months later, I come out screeching, and they think the sound is heavenly."

I glare at the sliver still stuck in my finger.

"Do you want coffee or something? Come, sit down. What do you take?"

"Cinnamon." I sink into the sofa's damp cushions.

Try to suck the sliver from my finger.

Thea turns inside. She's going to want to know my name. Tabitha curls around my ankles.

The woman returns, hands me a mason jar mug, the cinnamon settled into a lump at the bottom. And a pair of tweezers.

"Thanks."

"No worries, hun."

"Robin." That's what the cop named Carson. Robin Hood.

"That's a pretty name. Your mom choose it? Do you need a hand getting that out?"

"No. She doesn't have much to do with me."

"I'm sorry." Thea lights another cigarette, and I pluck the sliver.

Her cement blocks are cool on my feet, the coffee mug warm between my legs. What's more caffeine, now that I know it fuels my delusion?

My first real evening with this part of my family. Uncle Roy picked up Dacy from a friend's house after work, and they got home only a few minutes before my aunt. Dacy said I couldn't wear PJs for dinner, especially ones with dirt on the ass, so she found me a pair of leggings and a T-shirt. Didn't ask what I did all day, how I got so dirty. I changed just as Aunt Jocelyn came through the door. Probably for the best—don't want her thinking I'm completely incapable of living.

They do family dinners, it seems. We all sit at the table, a formidable square, wooden with no marks on the surface. Store-bought rotisserie chicken in the centre, next to one of those bagged salads that come with the dressing and everything. Uncle Roy mixed the romaine and croutons together in a bowl while Dacy set the table. My aunt had stopped at the store to buy the ingredients, shouted something about wanting leftovers for tomorrow's lunch, before she went upstairs to take off her tights and pencil skirt. I sat at the table, unsure of my place in this routine. When my aunt came back down, everyone took their places at the table and started dishing up. Salad first, still-warm chicken on top. I copy them, take as little as possible in case I haven't been figured into the routine—in case there isn't enough for their lunches tomorrow.

"How was everyone's day? Dacy, how was school?" My aunt, her fork poised over her plate.

Uncle Roy and I munch in silence, not answering because the question wasn't really addressed to us.

"All right. I didn't go to French again." She shrugs, and her shirt slips farther down her shoulder.

"Dacy," my aunt's voice scolds.

"We had that sub, you know, the one who just makes us watch weird movies and tells us stories about his dogs."

Uncle Roy interjects, "You can't have too many absences. It looks bad on your report card."

"Did either of you get a call today? I went for attendance, then left, and he didn't even notice."

My aunt sets down her fork, "I don't want you to get into the habit of missing class." Bacon bits and creamy dressing visible on her tongue as she talks.

"It's not like it's even important. I go to all my sciences." Dacy stabs a piece of lettuce with her fork.

"Good girl." Uncle Roy smiles. "Wish I could sneak out of the office some days. Today wasn't so bad, meetings all afternoon, so at least I got away from the computer."

My aunt joins back in. "Lucky. I was shackled to my desk all day." She rolls her shoulders for emphasis.

I sit at the back table in French class. No desks, just table groups like elementary school. French needs to be interactive. The closest my group comes to notetaking is doodling our own representations of French words and snickering about them. A bloated face coughing a spiky hairball for *avec*, flowers in a tacky vase for *avoir*.

Devin encouraged French class so we could get by in Paris. It didn't help. Though once I did manage to order *une tarte framboise, s'il te plaît*? But I used the informal *you*, and the woman taking my order got offended. Her lips pursed tight as she thrust my dessert over the counter.

Hand on fork, fork to mouth. We all chew, mashing chicken, croutons. The chicken's good and salty, but the salad could use more dressing. They don't give enough in the proportioned packs. I reach for the pepper. Too far.

"Can you pass the pepper?" I squeak, unsure of drawing attention to myself.

Dacy passes it and the salt.

"How was your day?" Uncle Roy looks at me, remembering I'm here.

"Good, I met one of your neighbours."

"Sarah across the way? She's pretty good about stopping to talk." My aunt scrapes her fork along her plate to catch the last of the parmesan.

"No, Thea."

She squints at her plate. "Thea?"

"Her back yard faces yours. She's got an outdoor sofa."

Dacy's lips flatten together, eyebrows raise like she's trying not to laugh.

"The lady who mows her weeds? She's never spoken to us." My aunt places her cutlery over the plate diagonally. A small clink as the knife and fork meet. Just like that, dinner is over.

I'm designated to wash dishes while Dacy dries and puts away, because "you don't know the cupboards yet," she says. There is a dishwasher, but only for forks and plates, which have to be rinsed anyway. The pan from fried eggs this morning should have been soaked earlier. Cheese, melted on top, thinks it's part of the metal and non-stick coating. I don't remember having breakfast. Or any other meal today. My stomach gurgles, even though we just finished eating.

"Since you aren't doing anything during the day, do you think you could help make dinners?" Sitting at the island, glass of white wine, my aunt looks at me.

Mother's Day before my mom left. I had no money and no job, just finishing Grade 9, and freshly done with my group therapy sessions. At the beginning, I had to go every day, but by the end of the six months it was down to one session each week. Instead of the usual sit-in-a-group and talk type thing they show on TV, my weekly sessions were structured as cooking classes. My group was for "troubled individuals who do not show signs of self-harm or of wishing to harm others," meaning we could be trusted around knives. We learned a new meal each week, and talked about how cooking is like meditating and can be a method of communicating how much we love and appreciate someone when we can't find the right words. Lessons were Tuesdays after school.

My Mother's Day gift was a dinner. Cooked with all my love and apologies.

Nathan, Nate, a graduate of our program, wore a white apron and jeans, hairnet under his ball cap, and never spilled anything on himself. The apron was part of the presentation. He taught us to measure, follow recipes. Terry, a girl a few years older than me, always wanted to experiment, add something new. Cumin, mostly. "Because it smells like male pheromones after sex," she told me once. But the recipe is "tried and true." Tried and true.

At home I didn't have any recipes, no cookbooks, just memories of the lessons when I was Terry's kitchen partner and our dishes never turned out quite right. But she wasn't there to drag me down, so I knew I'd excel. Really surprise my mom.

Chicken cordon bleu. My dad bought the ingredients. I pounded the chicken breasts flat between wax paper with a hammer, but the paper ripped, and the chicken got a bit mushed. Rolled the ham and swiss inside, dusted with flour, then dipped the chicken breasts in milk and coated with breadcrumbs. I made roasted potatoes and asparagus and béarnaise sauce from the package. Too much cumin in the potatoes. Too much balsamic on the asparagus. And the béarnaise sauce broke, separated. Too much butter, even though I followed the directions on the package.

I displayed the meal on Mom's best china with the silver cutlery I forgot to polish.

Mom, Dad, and I sat down. My back straight, leaning forward, I watched her take a bite. Mom chewed slowly.

"Well, no one's going to say you undercooked the chicken." Swallow. "But everything looks lovely."

I tried some, and the breast crumbled to ash on my tongue, her words caught between my teeth. That was the only bite I ate. Dad finished his plate and Mom left half. "It's just too much for me, next time smaller portions. And set the oven timer."

She left before I finished that school year. Took her china plates and silver cutlery.

I didn't cook again. Not from memory, not from a recipe, tried and true.

My hands soapy, frozen, holding the cheesy-eggy pan. "Anything particular?"

"Just find something in the freezer." She gulps half her wine, refills her glass, and leaves the kitchen.

I have to pass Dacy's room to get to mine—Devin's. Upstairs all the doors are closed, even the bathroom, though there's no light coming from underneath. I left Devin's door open, but it's shut too. The hallway, intimidating in its varying shades of beige: walls, floorboards, carpet, and doors. Turn to go back downstairs, maybe sit on the sofa with my uncle. Watch a sitcom.

"Hey, I thought I heard you. Come in." Dacy opens her door, light reflects from her lilac walls and spills across the carpet.

"Nice room."

Dirty clothes heaped over the floor. Bed rumpled and littered with magazines and textbooks. A dresser, drawers dangling open with more clothes spewing from their confines.

"Thanks. When did you last do a facial? I'm just about to put on a mask."

"Um." What?

I catch my reflection in her full-length mirror. Yeah, my face still looks like shit. Acne and that cut where I tried to pop one. Bags under my eyes. One good night's sleep isn't enough to undo all the damage.

"Here, tie your hair up, and let's see what we can do. Getting pretty always makes me feel better." Her hair's pulled back with a workout headband, skin clear and make-up free. She looks painfully young.

"Thanks." I take the offered hair elastic.

Dacy sits me in her desk chair, rubs a damp pad over my face. It burns over the hole I tore yesterday.

"You've got to cleanse first, then apply the face mask." She kneels in front of me, squeezes a thick pink paste from a pouch. Dabs it on my face, spreading in circles. Finished, she turns to her mirror and does the same to her face. "While we wait, I'm going to fix your brows."

A hand with painted nails moves toward me, tweezers ready. I have an urge to grab them, force them into my eye. Dacy's eyes narrow, concentrating. One hand under my chin to keep me still. Her breath smells like mint, lips move slightly. She's chewing gum.

"How long are you staying?" She asks, her face so close to mine I can only see her pink smeared cheek, chin.

"I don't know. Why?"

"It's nice, you here. Kind of like I have an older sister again." She rips hairs from between my eyebrows, and my eyes sting with tears.

BACK YARD

On the deck again, I'm smoking when Dacy comes out holding two mugs and two slices of toast with jam.

I take a coffee with my free hand. "Thanks." Sip it. I don't let the coffee touch my tongue—don't try to discern the taste or trick myself into liking it. I'm here for the caffeine buzz. The comforting suggestion that Devin could be around any corner.

Beside me, Dacy puts everything on the table and pulls out a cigarette. Lights it on the first try.

"I thought you wanted to be a doctor?"

"So?" Eye roll. Inhale. "Nothing beats a cigarette with coffee on a cool morning."

"Devin didn't smoke."

"She did when she was my age. Before she got shipped off to live with you. She did other things, too."

Dinner. Find something in the freezer. Which freezer? Fridge freezer or deep freezer in the basement? Both only have frost-bitten meats and five-minute dinners. I take out all the alfredo sauce dinners, penne and fettuccine noodles, and a bag of ground beef.

Standing at the stove, hands on my hips, I survey my ingredients. Meagre. But there are lots of spices in the cupboard. I microwave the ground beef first, but forget to put the bag in a bowl, and the juices leak all over. Leave the mess until I'm done microwaving everything. I put two dinners in. Rummage through drawers to find a pan, toss the beef in and set the stove on medium. Oregano, thyme, nutmeg, poultry seasoning, and garlic powder. I try to strain the grease into the sink and lose some beef with it. The microwave beeps. It's been beeping for a while now.

Hotter than I expect, I drop the alfredo dish on the counter. Splats across the pan. I lift the soggy cardboard and pour the microwave "dinner" into the pan, it falls in a chunk, the sauce and pasta globbed together. Follow it with the other and turn up the heat. Fry the pasta with the beef. Use a spatula to hack apart the semi-frozen alfredo chunks and end up accidentally splashing myself with the greasy sauce. Some of the noodles stick to the bottom of the pan. Start to burn, so I stir faster, add a spoonful of butter.

I should make garlic bread. There's some whole wheat sandwich bread in the cupboard, I sprinkle some garlic powder on top, and stick it in the toaster.

KITCHEN

Table set. Waiting, waiting.

I'm lying on the couch, whining about a sore throat. Barely able to make enough noise to continue whining. Devin comes into the room with a damp cloth. Pats my face with it and leaves it across my forehead.

She flicks my nose. "You get better now. I'm sick of looking after you!"

But Devin's smiling, and I know she doesn't mind too much. I start coughing. Coughing. I don't cover my mouth. So violent, I hold myself. An attempt to prevent my coughs from bursting through my chest. Devin comes to hold me too. Strokes my sticky hair behind my ears, wraps my head in her arms.

I don't notice her bitten cuticle, on her thumb, skin ripped from the nail to knuckle. Open.

"Hello! Something smells interesting!" My uncle booms, I hear his boots slam, then the door.

"Need a hand?" Dacy races to my side.

"I think I'm okay. Unless, should we butter the garlic bread?"

"Definitely. Did you make garlic butter?"

I move slower, putting the toast on a plate. "I used garlic powder."

"Oh, well, that'll be good too."

We all sit around the table, except Aunt Jocelyn. She's staying late at work. Dacy told me this happens a few times a week.

"How was everyone's day?" Dacy assumes her mother's position at the table, looks at me first.

Nobody makes eye contact with me. They swirl the grey sauced grey beef and bloated noodles, tear the bread into pieces and leave them littered on their plates.

"This, this is really something, right, Dace? Never had something quite like this."

"I was told to look in the freezer."

Dacy's doing homework, physics, at the kitchen table now that we've cleared away dinner. Uncle Roy's surfing channels. The kitchen and living room bleed into each other, so I think I should be in one or the other, not hiding upstairs or outside.

I dash to my—Devin's—room and pull out my book, then run back to the kitchen. I don't know why, but I can't seem to finish. Reading and flipping pages, and never getting any closer to the last page, the unveiling. Where does Arachne end? I feel like the researcher, the searcher, the questioner. Asking where she went. What happened? Over and over, and I know it's more than just this character, but Devin, too. I don't want to know if she's gone for good.

Uncle Roy turns off the TV and tosses the remote on the coffee table with a bang. "Anyone else need an evening snack?"

"Sure!" says Dacy.

I don't answer. Dinner's roiling in my stomach. I was the only one who ate. Forced mouthfuls down out of spite and wished I could have stared at my aunt as I did. As if to say, this is what you get for asking me to cook. But, of course, she isn't home yet.

My uncle finds a few blocks of cheese, boxes of crackers, and dill pickles. Cuts them into bite-sized slices and arranges them on two plates, one for Dacy, one for himself.

"You going to come sit with me? Not like I'll finish all this myself." He winks at me.

"Do you guys do this often?" I follow him to the couch.

"Snacks?"

I move a throw pillow out of my way. "Sitting around all together in the evening."

"Most nights, right, Dace? Mom goes to bed early, but we stay up."

"Did Devin stay up?" I trace the gold circle on the throw pillow with my finger.

Uncle Roy takes a noisy bite of a cracker.

"Sorta. Devin never did homework." Dacy speaks, breaks the pause.

"She liked crime shows. All of them. A different one every night." The first time I've heard my uncle talk about Devin.

I laugh, remembering. "Oh yeah, *CSI*, *Criminal Minds*, *NCIS*, she made me watch all of them. Even convinced Dad to get a different cable package so she could watch them."

Dacy brings her snack to the living room and joins us. "Mom didn't like me watching those shows, but Dad let me stay up with them." She munches a pickle and continues, "You always said life's short, gotta spend time with those you love."

Dacy stares at her lap as her words settle in a blanket over us.

I could mention that I was taught that aphorism in group therapy, but I don't. We let our chewing fill the room. Uncle Roy turns on the TV and finds an episode of *Criminal Minds*. It's a rerun I watched with Devin, curled on the couch beside her. I haven't seen any of the new episodes. At home, I get annoyed when watching crime shows. All the scenes in the morgues irritate me. Kramer and I didn't run tests or anything, so I don't know how accurate those are, but I've seen enough dead bodies to know what they look like. How long it takes for the skin to change colour, eyes to sink. Then again, no one would want to watch a show with real dead bodies. Everyone likes to cling to their illusions.

Shadows of trees and creatures cast by the streetlamp slink across the carpet, bedspread, reach for me. The single shoot of bamboo glows dimly. Sways in the breeze.

"Why are you here?" Devin, sitting on the windowsill. She must have climbed the trellis outside.

Her legs dangle. Tree branch phantoms rustle her hair, long and straight. Crooked nose and one eyebrow raised just like in the pictures.

"I miss you."

"Then why aren't you looking for me?"

"You're right here."

"No."

I stretch toward her, let the shadows prick my skin. Devin smiles, lips together, and I realize I forgot how she smiles. Forgot how just one side curves up and the eyebrow on the same side also swings up. Up and up. How her front tooth bites her lower lip, her eyes glancing to the ground.

I move to stand, unwrap my legs from the blanket. Devin slides off the ledge, walks to me. She stands between my legs, both our thighs touching, and I notice she's wearing the bathrobe from our water fight. The collar speckled with blood, still red, though so many years old. I place my hands on her lower back, and Devin presses me close. Her fingers over my shoulders, thumbs on my collarbone. I glance down, and though I can feel her touching me with both hands, she only has one.

She's not cold. Rather, like the breeze through the window. Fluid, more like lukewarm water than anything. Holding her, feeling the ridges on her spine, I know. I know. I can smell her, the weird salt of the ocean in the middle of the prairies. And that's not how she smells at all. I'm in her hospital room, hand against the windowpane, looking at the waves. Crashing on the sand, carrying my fingerprints. Except she didn't have an ocean view. And I was next to Devin the whole time, not looking out her window to the parking lot and rain. Her hands in mine and her eyes closed. Her fingers black, and the black spreading over her wrist, up her arm.

But now, now she's exactly as she was. After the amputation. Able to move and feel and grasp. Even if no one else can see.

"I miss you." Devin kisses my forehead.

I wake when the sky's coloured grey with a strained light. Tinted orange from a weak sun. Cold air breathes on my eyelashes, and for a moment I hope Devin crawled into bed with me. That if I were to turn, I'd see her, asleep, hand under her cheek. But Devin never came to me. When nightmares wouldn't vanish when I opened my eyes, I would go to her. Through her door, softly, softly and find a place next to her.

But I'm already in her room.

I blink and roll over. Maybe she could be here. My arm finds a body, warm, next to me. Dark hair snarled with itself. I stroke the strands, move them off her face, behind her ear. Dacy. She snores, just a little. Quiet, I ease out of bed. Make sure to tuck the comforter around her shoulders.

At the door, I turn back. The window, bamboo branch, and small body curled asleep. I think I should whisper something, make her nightmares disappear. But I can't. I don't know how.

I sit on the deck. Don't realize I've lit a cigarette until it's half ash, dropping between my fingers, the cherry a weak mirror of the rising sun. Pink and purple streaks lighten the heavy clouds, preceding the orange globe's arrival. . Watery, it dazzles the ropes of dew strung on spider webs. Outside, looking in, I watch my aunt make breakfast for Dacy and my uncle. Watch without really looking, just peripheral glances. No one calls me to eat. I'm not hungry. They bring their dishes to the counter and turn off the lights.

Behind me, a door opens.

"I thought you might be cold." Dacy offers a blanket.

Her hair now tied in a messy bun, another blanket wrapped around her. She lights a cigarette with me. Her parents must've already left for work—she wouldn't smoke in front of them.

"Thanks."

We smoke in silence, and she leaves. I hear movement in the kitchen behind me, but faint. Dacy, probably packing her lunch, organising homework. I don't want to talk to anyone, and she doesn't return to bother me.

Tabitha saunters across the top of the fence to say hello when the house quiets and the sun is full. She hops onto the deck and rubs her face on my calves, against the metal chair leg.

Purring, Tabitha hops onto my lap. Kneads her paws on my tits and meows like I'm not paying attention to her.

Thea steps onto her makeshift patio and waves at me. I lift my hand in a half salute before turning inside. Tabitha stalks away, tail in the air.

Dressed in borrowed leggings and the same T-shirt as yesterday, I come back outside and vault the fence to Thea's yard. Actually, I trample my aunt's flower bed and somehow bash my nose while trying to clamber over the fence. I manage to get on top, topple over, and wind myself on a sofa cushion Thea strategically placed for me.

"I see you decided to get dressed before attempting acrobatics this morning."

"Do you know how to cook?" I jog over to her sofa and settle beside Tabitha.

She sips her coffee slow. "Depends what you want to make."

"Anything." I pant, still trying to catch my breath, "I have to make dinner, and last night was inedible."

"What do you have to work with?" Thea doesn't laugh at me, the wrinkles on her face soft.

"A freezer full of grey meat and canned vegetables."

"Let me get dressed. We're going grocery shopping."

Thea and I spend over an hour at the store, finding everything for curry chicken. I've never made any type of curry before, so it's a good thing that she's going to walk me through all the steps once we get back to her place. She whipped out her credit card and paid before I could say I didn't bring my wallet. Probably noticed my outfit doesn't have pockets and I left my bag at my aunt's, but all Thea says is "need to collect those airmiles." Then we're driving back to her place, Thea's driving, I'm in the passenger seat. Windows rolled down because the late April sun is stifling, and she doesn't have air conditioning. It's not even five degrees out, but the sun is direct on the windshield.

"Stop for ice cream?" Thea swerves through an intersection to a drive-thru.

"Sure, swirl?"

"Good call." She leans toward the metal voice box, "Two swirl cones." Before the person inside has the chance to greet us.

"That's gonna be one dollar and twelve cents. Unless you want to tip me, which would be sweet, because I've got a contest with the other drive-girl and she's got more tips so far."

We both laugh. Thea opens her wallet, scrounges the bottom and finds a five as she pulls forward.

The girl, younger than Dacy and with feathers dangling from her earrings, passes the cones, then yelps when she sees how much Thea gave her. "Thank you so much! Now I'm defs ahead!"

I snort into my ice cream. Thea bites hers.

My sunglasses dye the sky and grass and road sepia. I'm in the passenger seat with ice cream, and I've only ever had ice cream at the wheel. With Frank and the others who sat in the van's passenger seat with my sunglasses over their eyes.

"Don't let the milk boil over."

"It's not even bubbling."

Thea's kitchen is different from Aunt Jocelyn's. Bigger, counters cluttered with vitamin containers; recipe books; two bottles of wine, one empty; a fancy espresso maker. She had to clear away some dishes of nuts and candies to make space for the cutting board. Flat stovetop has a ring of something charred around the largest burner, but I'm using the small one for the coconut-milk mixture. Two cups of milk, one of shredded coconut, because Thea says coconut milk from the can doesn't taste as good. She cubes the chicken into pieces smaller than playing dice. Nice and bite sized.

"Can you grab the flour from the pantry and put the butter in the deep pot?"

I open the pantry door. It's a walk-in, four feet deep and stocked from floor to ceiling.

"Where is the flour?"

"Clear container, red lid. Right side, middle shelf."

All the containers on the right middle shelf are clear with red lids. Six have white ingredients inside. I lift the lids: baking powder or soda, salt or sugar, flour? I pull out the second largest container.

"This?"

"No, the other one. That's icing sugar." She browns the chicken in a pan beside my pot.

"How can you tell?"

"The flour's in the big container."

A sloppy sizzling sound interrupts my reply.

"Shit, Robin. Get the milk!" Thea removes her pan from the stove and steps out of my way.

I hesitate a moment, frantically looking for a bird, then remember my name. White foam engulfs the pot, milk streaming out and across the stove. I grab the handle, hold the pot over the sink. Thea, still holding her hot pan in one hand, wipes the mess with a cloth. Quick, efficient. A sludgy half ring forms, similar to the one around the larger burner.

"What now?"

"Strain the milk."

Thea passes me a sieve and a one litre Pyrex measuring cup for the coconut milk. Thea melts the butter and adds a bit of flour in the large pot.

"You could put onions in, but my kids always picked them out, so I stopped."

The coconut perfumes the kitchen. "Your kids?"

"Taidgh and Marjolaine, little Lainey I called her."

"Did they live here too?"

"Until the divorce. Can you pour the chicken broth and milk into my flour paste?" Thea gestures at the carton of broth, and I'm glad we strained the coconut milk into a container with a spout and handle instead of a bowl—the glass is too hot to touch.

Stir until the lumps dissolve. Add chicken, and shrimp or turkey or scallops—if we had any. Lid on and stove turned to low.

"My cousin, Devin, she used to live around here too. But then she lived with me. Her mom didn't want her, so my dad took her in."

"I wouldn't have given up my kids for the world." Thea lifts the lid and stirs. "They chose their father."

"Did they ever know Devin? Her sister still lives over there. Dacy."

"Taidgh's at school though, now, out on his own. Nearly done his second year of geoengineering in Saskatchewan."

"Maybe he knew Devin? She was here five, no six, years ago. When were you divorced?"

"Seven years this past spring."

"What about Lainey?"

"She's in high school. Graduating this year."

"But did she know the kids in the neighbourhood? Before she left?"

"A few. Yes, Dacy, the little girl with long pigtail braids. She would knock on the door, always so polite, and ask for Lainey.

They liked to annoy the boys. Run away with their soccer balls, that sort of thing."

I lift the lid and stir. Curry thickening.

"Of course, before long the boys were too old for playing in front of our house. They would go to the mall instead. Lainey and her friend wanted to tag along, but I never let them."

"Lainey must've left around the same time as Devin."

"The older sister? I never saw much of her. Where is she now?"

"I don't know."

"Dacy stood on my front steps one day. She knocked, asked for Lainey, and I had to tell her Lainey moved. I offered her tea, poor girl was shaking. Red faced and teary eyed, just trying to figure out why her friend was gone. Haven't seen her since, except in glances when we're both in our back yards."

Thea shows me how to make rice. Double the amount of water to rice, we measure using her mason jar mugs. When everything's ready, she puts it in clean, plastic yogurt containers. The containers go into a plastic grocery bag.

"Robin, put the rice in the bowls first, curry on top. Serve with nuts or tinned pineapple, if you have any, if you want."

I nod, and we both exit through the back door. Have a final cigarette after our cooking day.

"It's been wonderful. You being here today. I don't get out much, thank you."

"Thank you. Sure you don't want any dinner?"

"No, no. I'm fine." She stubs her cigarette.

Thea leans in, hugs me with both her arms. One hand on my shoulder, one my lower back. Cheek pressed into my forehead, hair, her nose at my ear.

"I should be going."

We detach. Disengage. I heft the grocery bag, walk to the fence.

"Here, you get up, and let me pass you the dinner once you're over." Thea doesn't advise me to walk around the block, out the front door.

"Yeah, sounds like the best plan."

I step onto a small rock and bounce to propel myself over. Thea's backyard is lower, the fence higher. Tabitha meows from the top, urges me up. Four tries, and I get purchase. Leg up, over, down. No falling this time.

Rummaging through the cupboards, I find two pots, one large, one not. Same, similar, to Thea's. Rice in the small pot, curry in the other. Heat on low, fill the sink with soapy water and wash the cutting board and knives I didn't use. Yogurt containers rinsed and recycled. I'm still not used to Calgary's recycling program and have to remind myself not to separate the plastics from glass from tins. Just one blue bin where I bury Thea's yogurt tubs under brown paper bags and empty wine bottles so they aren't suspiciously on top. Dacy and her dad come home at the same time again, as I casually stir the creamy sauce. Still thickening.

"Something smells good!"

"Almost ready."

My uncle flings his coat over the back of a bar stool, "Smells really good."

"I followed a recipe."

Dacy bumps my hip with hers before pulling down the plates. "Good choice. Last night's mush was terrible." Three plates.

"Dace! Be polite, it was only questionable." Uncle Roy winks at us.

"Do you have any nuts?"

"Maybe cashews in the pantry. Not sure."

I find bowls under the counter, pour the curry into the clear one, rice into the orange. The curry doesn't all fit into the serving bowl, so I leave some on the stove.

"You mixed up the bowls." Dacy says.

"What?"

"The clear is the rice bowl. Always has been. See how it doesn't fill the orange?"

I stand with my hands on my hips. "So?"

"The rice goes in the rice bowl."

"I think we can forgive her not knowing about the rice bowl, Dace. Here, put the cashews in a dish."

"Is there a cashew dish I should know about?" I roll my eyes and put the dirty pots into the soapy sink.

We set the table, all together. My aunt doesn't come home, and no one comments on her absence. The creamy curry sauce seeps into the rice, and we eat without much conversation. No one needs a distraction from this meal. Cashews crunch between my teeth. No leftovers.

After dinner, Uncle Roy retreats to his study, a small desk wedged in a loft area upstairs overlooking the driveway. He said he didn't finish all his work for the day, had to bring some home because he picked up Dacy from Heritage Station after school.

I'm sitting on the counter, swinging my legs. "What's up with your mom?"

"Nothing, she's got a board meeting for the community centre tonight." Dacy scrubs the curry pot.

"But no one talked about her at dinner."

"Should we?"

I shrug, hop off the counter, and put our unrinsed cutlery in the dishwasher.

"She won't be home until late." Dacy arranges the cleaned pots in one half of the sink and rummages through the tea towel drawer, apparently searching for a specific towel. She retrieves a thick cloth and begins drying the pots.

"Devin always complained about her mom being home all the time."

"And then Devin died." Dacy throws her cloth in the soapy water and stalks upstairs. I drain the sink and wring out the soaking tea towel.

I turn to the coffee maker. Can't be too hard to make a cup.

Water first. Coffee needs water and beans. A flap on the back hides the place for water. I bring the machine beside the sink and pull the movable faucet to fill the hole. Next, I look for coffee. Find it in the bottom drawer beside the oven. Four different types, all open: Starbucks Kenya, Kicking Horse Grizzly Claw, Salt Spring Island Blue Heron, and New Orleans blend. Dacy's favourite. Why do they need four flavours of coffee? There's only three family members.

The beans are whole. I see a grinder on the counter, at least, I think it's a grinder. Heavy and stainless steel with too many buttons and a knob. I open drawers at random, looking for an instruction manual until I find a hammer. That'll do. I remember my hammer-chicken-waxed paper debacle. Wrap the beans in a clean tea towel and lump them on the cutting board. Hammer on wood makes the sound of insects being squished underfoot. I stop pulverising the coffee before Uncle Roy comes downstairs to ask what I'm doing.

Under the towel, only half the beans are cracked open, and a fine, brown powder velcros itself to the fabric. On the coffee maker, I locate the button to release the place for the beans, scoop them into my hands, and pour them in. The front of the machine has six more buttons, little line drawings to indicate which is which. Circle with a *v* inside for the clock, I assume. Fancy but indiscernible markings probably for timers or amount. I push the one with the typical power-button symbol. A light flashes blue, and a gurgling comes from inside the machine.

Once brewed, the coffee looks a bit weak. Thin, reddish brown liquid when I hold the pot up to the light. I rummage for a mug. One has a small chip on the inside lip. I pour Dacy's coffee into it.

Tea's much easier.

I don't knock. "Hi."

"Hi." Dacy's on her bed, legs crossed, textbook open.

"Science?"

"Chem. I have a test on organic chemistry equations this week."

"I made you coffee." Still holding the mug like it's mine. One hand on the handle, the other cradling the bottom.

She reaches for it. Takes a sip. "Thanks."

I sit on the end of her bed. How do you talk to a sister?

"Mom's out with William. They've been seeing each other since—a while ago. After the funeral."

I wish I had poured myself a coffee, just to have the mug to fidget with. "Does your dad know?"

"Probably. Pretending's better. He worked a lot before Devin left, and then even more when she couldn't come home."

"I'm sorry."

"Why? She's happy." Dacy brings the mug to her lips. "This coffee is shit."

We sit in silence for a while—I don't know how long. Dacy doesn't have a clock, and I don't move to check my phone for the time. She sips her coffee, and I can see her teeth on the inside of her mug, probably trying to strain out the chunks of beans floating in the mixture.

"So," Dacy says, and I realize I'm biting a hangnail on my thumb. "What about you?"

I fold my hands together. "What about me?"

"Dating anyone? Or something more scandalous?" She grins and puts her empty mug on the side table. Dregs of beans coat the inside, and I wish I could read tea leaves. Tell her fortune. Reassure her that life gets better, even though I don't how much truth there is to that cliché. Of course, these aren't tea leaves. Coffee grounds would probably lie. I shake my head.

"No, nothing. Well, I don't know, the guy I was with on the road, we had a moment."

"Oh my god! The car thief? Details."

My aunt or uncle must've told her about Carson. "I gave him a hand job in the car. That's all." Does this count as TMI? How much do you share? Devin gave me all the details, right down to circumcised or not, but I've never shared anything. I didn't have any stories before her.

"Like, while he was driving?"

"No, I was."

Dacy shuts her textbook and makes space for me to sit cross-legged on her bed, facing her. "That sounds dangerous."

"And before him, there was a girl I met at a party."

"Oooh, you go both ways, then? Or were you, like, just trying to see, maybe? I kissed a girl once, but I don't think I could ever date another girl. What if she were the pretty one of the couple? Like, come on, I can't deal with that stress!" Dacy laughs.

"Well, actually, he was kind of the experiment." Pause. "Guys scare me." I whisper.

"That's silly. A guy is supposed to protect you."

I don't tell her about Devin and Collin. About the fire, and the guy I can barely remember, and how my mom left. Drugged drinks and consequences. If she doesn't already know, then she will. Or maybe she has to pretend she doesn't know. Has to play the pretty fool.

"Anyway, sounds like traditional relationships aren't really your thing." Dacy picks up her mug, looks at the false tea leaves. Puts it back as if she saw a future she didn't want.

"People don't stay, and I'm tired of being left behind. I'd rather be the one to peace out."

"How sad. Even my mom and dad, neither of them leaves. I think it would be nice to have someone you always come back to."

I run my hand through my hair and find a twig, probably from hopping the fence into Thea's yard this morning. "Isn't this William guy a type of leaving?"

"No." Dacy opens her textbook cover, then shuts it. "No. I've only dated one person, ever. Am dating. He's nice, and he sometimes sleeps with other girls, but he doesn't leave me."

"But you—you don't see anyone else? Why not?"

Dacy barks a short laugh. "I know, it would only be fair! But no. I'm too busy with school. I've got to keep up my marks so I can apply to universities next year. And I'm looking for a summer job, and spending time with friends and you. I don't want to deal with more than one guy."

I nod, "Fair enough."

"Maybe you've got the right idea. Non-relationships or women. Now that I think about it, both seem like less effort."

"Love takes effort but shouldn't feel like it does." Words from my past, from the group therapy, conjure themselves.

"Easy for you to say, miss I-only-leave-people."

KITCHEN

Uncle Roy calls us downstairs. He put out bowls of vanilla ice cream for us. Spread sprinkles and chocolate sauce and chopped bananas in dishes over the counter.

"Time for a break. Too much work makes you crazy."

"Thanks, Dad. There's coffee, too." Dacy pours herself another cup.

"I already got some." He raises his mug. "Not sure how I feel about the grounds floating at the bottom."

I cross my arms, defensive. "I don't own a coffee maker."

"Next time use a filter before adding the grinds," Dacy says. "But good effort."

They both smile at me. Uncle Roy douses his ice cream in chocolate sauce and tops it with a single banana slice.

Sundaes made, we gather on the couch. Uncle Roy turns on the TV. *CSI: Miami*, the worst one. No one complains. I mix my sprinkles into the ice cream, swirling rainbow colours until the whole thing turns purple-brown and starts melting.

I wake early. Put on a hoodie, cigarettes and lighter in the pocket. The kitchen dim, but the stove light on, and my aunt chopping vegetables. Quiet.

She speaks without looking at me. "I didn't think you'd be up so early."

"How was your date last night?"

The knife hovers just a little too long, poised.

"You talked to Dacy."

"Is William a secret?" I stand with my hands on the counter, across from her.

She still won't look at me. "Why do you care?"

"Why do you stay?"

She stops chopping. Mimics how I lean. Her hand still on the knife.

"Because I'm a mom."

I withdraw from the counter. Curl my arms around myself. "Moms don't stay."

"I'm not your mom." She takes a deep breath, resumes dicing her cucumber. "Phil wanted me to come out right after. You'd just been released, and your father was so stressed. Thought having more maternal figures around would be good. For both you and your mom."

"But you didn't come." I bring my thumb to my mouth. Bite my hangnail.

"Devin, she needed me home."

"Bullshit. You sent her to us at the end of the school year."

My aunt moves her jaw, her neck muscles straining. She blinks fast, like something's caught in her eye, dust or memories or a stray eyelash. My fingers tremble, and I shove through the door to the back deck.

Dacy didn't smoke with me this morning, but she always expects me in the evening. After dinner—after I've muddled through a recipe or, more likely, gone to Thea's and followed her instructions. After I make it look like I've cooked for hours, then we stack the dishes in the washer, and Dacy goes to study. Sometimes at the kitchen table, sometimes in her room. I hang out with Uncle Roy, which means that we watch crappy TV and suffer through commercial breaks by complaining about the shows we watch. After an episode or two, I make tea for Dacy and myself, and we sit on her bed. Legs stretched out, backs on her pillows. I ease into this routine like I'm lowering myself into a warm bath. Comfortable. Familiar.

"How was Paris?" Dacy, painting her nails, doesn't look at me.

"What do you mean?"

She swipes the copper polish over her pinkie nail, just a thin layer. "Devin, she couldn't stop talking about it when she got back. The café across from the Louvre, she said it was her favourite place. So much bustle and talk, even though she couldn't understand the words. I can't wait until I go."

"We liked to pretend we lived there. Pointing out stores and bridges and inventing memories of what we did there." I forgot we did that until now. Until I voiced it. Or is that only a memory I wish I had?

"My mom and I are going after I graduate. I want to go to all the places you two went. It sounds fantastic. You want pink or blue?" Dacy holds up the nail polish bottles. Doesn't offer the copper.

"Not your dad? Blue."

"No, it's going to be our girls' trip. Bonding. But I can't wait! Just another year and a bit." She takes my hand and applies the colour. "Anyway, what're you doing tomorrow?"

"Why?" Should've gone with pink. The blue reminds me of corpse nails. Cold and dead. I always painted them a pale pink before displaying them in their coffins, to give them the illusion of life. Perhaps the pink polish would've made me feel equally dead.

"Some friends and I are going out to see a show. Want to come?"

"You know, you're lucky."

"Yeah?" I look over at Devin.

Her face covered in a brown mask, circles around her mouth and eyes. Tweezers between her eyebrows as she leans toward the bathroom mirror.

"You only have one parent, and he's super cool. He's taking us to Europe. Neither of my parents would ever do that. Definitely not my dad."

"Why not?" Rubbing a home wax strip on the back of my thigh, foot on the ledge of the tub for a better angle.

"He's always working, doesn't have time to talk. I bet it was his idea to ship me off here."

"I'm glad you're here."

"Me too, but. But how much does your parent love you if he sends you away?"

I rip the strip off, gasp. Left it on too long. A reddish rectangular welt on my white skin.

"My parents tried to argue for juvie time or community service instead of the therapy. But then I ran away and they changed their minds." I apply a strip on my bikini line, right along my thong, "Although, then my mom left instead."

"They found my stash, and the next morning I was on a plane. It's funny though, my mom was thinking of getting a divorce, but then she and my dad united against me."

"Can you help me with this?"

Devin puts down the tweezers. One hand on my hip, the other on the strip. Rips up, hairs pulled out along with a thin layer of skin. She held the strip wrong, so the pain is greater than it should be. That doesn't matter—I will always trust her, even when it hurts.

This train Crowfoot, the intercom speaker declares as a C-train rumbles forward.

Round, green button flashes. Dacy jabs it, the doors glide apart. People sit, separated, quiet. Dacy finds a spot for us, but I hold the pole in the middle of the train instead. A lurch forward, pause, forward. Both hands on the yellow pole. Victoria doesn't have a train system, just buses.

She looks up at me, bright orange lipstick shaping her words. "Sure you don't want to sit?"

"I want to dance!" Out of the house, away from the confines of suburbia, I feel alive. Awake. Like I'd been sedated the last few weeks and finally the drugs have worn off. Clarity.

"Now?" Dacy digs through her bag. "You can dance at the bar."

On my toes, leaning back, arms stretched. I throw my body to one side, but the momentum of the train flings me around. Around.

Heritage Station. Please take all personal belongings when exiting the train.

Stop. My nose hits the pole. Dacy drops her open bag.

"Fuck! Are you okay?"

Blink, blink. Wrist under my nose, no blood. "Yeah, I'm good."

"Damn it. My stuff went everywhere!"

The train jerks forward again. I kneel, swipe my hands under the seat behind Dacy for her things. Lip gloss, compact mirror, keychain, loose nickels.

"Thanks!" she holds open her bag.

I pause, holding her keychain. One house key, a dangling letter D, a laser pointer. And a miniature Eiffel Tower. Silver, able to stand on its own.

IN REVERSE

Devin grips a keychain in her hand, skipping backwards. In the airport. We never saw the tower, not up close. We walked from a train station, lost ourselves in the streets. Found the river and the green stalls with scarves and paintings and cobblestones. Bread and coffee smells from the cafés opposite. The bridge with lovelocks. Where Dad took our photo. Pont des Arts. Hours, with the tower in the distance. Just a point we wandered toward. Devin smiling, laughing. And getting so close that the buildings one street further blocked the tower from view. But Dad got tired. Shin splints.

Devin bought the keychain to take the Eiffel with her.

Dacy hasn't noticed I still hold her keychain. She's lathering a shimmery lip gloss over the vibrant orange, making duck faces in her mirror. I slip Devin's tower off the ring.

Victoria Park Station.

I drop to my knees with the train's shudder. Throw Dacy's keychain, then pick it up again.

"You should really sit down."

"Yeah, that's probably a good plan." The tower safe in my pocket. "Found your keys."

Dacy leads us from the C-train station, through skyscrapers and apartment buildings. Rough stone on some, but mostly shiny glass and sharp corners. Not very different from Victoria, except taller. There's no ocean here. The air smells dead. A group of people stand on the sidewalk in front of a door.

"Hi! Grant, sorry I'm late. My cousin." Dacy gestures at me as she speaks to one of the guys in the group, "The train fascinated her. She's from a small town." She stands on tiptoes to kiss him, talking through their lips.

Ah, the totally not cheating boyfriend. She didn't mention he's obviously in his twenties. Probably older than me.

"Not that small." I glare. "The capital city of BC."

Grant looks over Dacy's head at me. "What are you guys on about? Vancouver is a massive city."

I ignore him and hide my eye roll by looking down—focus on lighting my cigarette.

"Anyway. What do I call you?" Beard, toque over his ears, two camera straps crossed over his chest. A typical hipster with a jailbait girlfriend.

Then again, who am I to judge? What's worse, an age gap or convenient hookups?

"Tonight? Lainey."

Dacy plucks a cigarette from Grant's front pocket. Leans over to me, "You use fake names at bars too? I'm always Devin, but that's because I have her old license."

Grant is talking to someone else. Another guy who looks almost identical, except he wears a union jack bandana instead of a toque. A haze of smoke drifts above our heads, all of us huddled like we're standing around a fire pit. Pink streaks across the sky seep between the buildings, despite the lateness.

"Isn't Devin's ID expired?"

"Yeah, but bars don't care if you're allowed to drive, only if you can drink."

Everyone tosses their stubs into the street at once. Worried about losing Dacy, I copy the others and throw my half-done cigarette on the growing pile. Inside, we immediately clamour down the stairs into a large and open basement. A stage off to the left, bar across the back. Dacy tells me the bands are "electro-funk, great for dancing."

And people are dancing. At the front, a circle of girls in tank tops and micro skirts. Hair puffed out so their heads appear too heavy for their bodies. Others, more like Keelie and Clive and Pigeon. Colours and layers and dreads. The outer ring is guys in plaid, jeans without rips, holding what I assume are craft beers and nodding their heads. Dacy wants to dance right away, but I head to the bar. My nose still stings from hitting it on the metal pole earlier.

"What can I get for you, pretty lady?" The bartender talks as he fills a drink.

What would Lainey drink?

He passes a vodka cran to a tank-top girl, waiting for my response.

"I'll have one of those." I gesture as the girl takes her drink and bounces away in a haze of hairspray and vanilla perfume.

"With just a twist of lime, right?" He turns away and starts making the drink before I agree.

Dacy perches beside me. "Any chance I can get a double Caesar? And two porn-star shots. Next one's on you."

We cheers our purple drinks, she whips her head back, lips parted, not spilling a drop. Bang our glasses on the bar.

"I knew a girl named Lainey, once."

"Really?"

"Totally forgot about her until I heard the name. She lived in the house behind ours. Then she didn't. I heard my parents talking to the neighbours. Lainey's mom lost her job, then just sat around at home. Never doing anything, so her husband left."

"Her name's Thea." I drink half my vodka cran in one gulp. Stand. Leave before I confess she made the curry. And the fettuccini, pulled pork, teriyaki salmon, jambalaya, chili, and other meals I've been serving for weeks.

Dacy's still at the bar. Grant's buying her drinks, she sits on his lap, fingers teasing his belt. So much for dancing. I edge into the boundary between the plaids and hippies. Part of me wants to scan the crowd for Devin, but I know it's futile. She died, I didn't. And if she were alive, she'd be pretty pissed at me for wasting so much time searching for her instead of enjoying life. I finish my drink and leave the empty glass on a random table. Wave at the bartender, and he pours me another as I weave back to the bar. Pass him a ten. Turn around—time to dance.

Rocking up and down, toes to heels, knees bent. The music's loud. Reverberates through the air, dissipates, stretches, and elongates. No one's thrashing their head. This band plays lower, for the hips down. Upper bodies moving only from momentum, from the crash of heels vibrating along calves, thighs, ribcages, and shoulders.

The girls at the front don't hear the music. They shriek and giggle above it, cameras flash like strobe lights. Out of step with the drums.

"Let's get closer!" Dacy screams in my ear. I can't see Grant anywhere.

She grabs my hand and threads us through the different rings, plunging side to side with the crowd and the music. We reach the stage. My hands fall onto its surface, waist high. Glasses with foam clinging to the bottom and electrical cords. The guitarist plays barefoot.

An ass jiggles against me, one of the vanilla and chemical scented girls. Tight. Everyone pressing forward. I swig my drink like it's a shot so I won't spill any in this crush of bodies. Leave the glass on top of the speaker beside me. Dacy yells with the singer, not any words, just mimicking the movement of his lips. Leaning over the stage, close, so close, my nose is almost against the singer's shin. Up, one leg and then the other, a smooth motion from all my fence-climbing practice, and I'm on the stage.

Still holding Dacy's hand, and she hops to sit on the stage, then stands, joins me. We spin, plant our feet, knees bent. The music sounds different up here. More jarring. My body, arms, find the rhythm. One shoulder pulls back, staccato, then the other, hips almost twerking. Dacy's head swings every way. Eye contact, and we dance close together, meshing our moves. The music, the energy, gets higher. Higher. I can barely see the crowd through the lights on us. But Pigeon. Her hair whips somewhere to the left, and I swear she's playing drums in the middle of the dancers. Pounding, pounding, and over again. I take Dacy by the chin, bring our mouths together. My tongue explores her teeth, probing. The crowd hollers louder, faster drums. Dacy's mouth opens, her tongue touches mine. Explodes.

Everything explodes. Dacy topples off stage, shatters the empty beer glasses like pine needles scattering. Ankle twisted in cords jerks the guitar. Screech as the guitarist is pulled off balance, his guitar unhooked. Stumbles onto the glass. Shard in his bare sole, but he yanks it out. Rights himself, his guitar. Starts to play, but the singer shouts to stop, stop!

On my knees, stage damp, fingers over the edge. Dacy. Her hair over her face, but her face on the ground. Ankle twisted in cords.

KITCHEN

"You're going home."

"I tried to be understanding. But taking Dacy to a bar. Phil. She's a bad influence."

Pause. The telephone murmurs. I'm on the couch, my aunt paces beside me. Uncle Roy's out with Dacy, picking up her prescription painkillers, so it's just the two of us here.

"You know what I went through with my first daughter. What your brother went through. I won't have it happen again." Glare. "Don't you dare try to turn this back on me. I'm not responsible for my daughters' behaviour."

Murmur, murmur. Hangs up. Slams her cell on the counter and watches it ring. *Phil—Home* lights up on the screen as the phone vibrates against the granite. Aunt Jocelyn ignores it.

"Your father's paying for a flight home. Pack. I'm driving you to the airport first thing in the morning."

Does no one remember that I'm an adult? I can fucking take care of myself.

I don't slam the door. Devin's door. I shut it, drag the end table in front of it. Almost drop the bamboo. Sitting, back against the foot of the bed, hard wood beam jutting into my shoulders. Closet door across from me closed. Plain white, two knob handles. I haven't opened it since I've been here. Think about getting up and pulling the knobs apart. Don't.

Fucking hell. I wish Devin were here. She would know how to deal with her mother. Or maybe she wouldn't. Maybe when Aunt Jocelyn gets an idea, she follows it through, no matter the consequences. Sent Devin away, now me. Has a steady boyfriend and a husband. Trying to make her fantasy world real. But whose fantasy wouldn't include Devin?

Carpet on my bare feet. Between my toes. Breaths come slower, slower. I rub my hands in the carpet, not soft, not prickly. Ground myself in the physicality of the moment. Get out of my head for a minute, like the therapists said. Without standing, I shimmy off my jeans—Dacy's jeans—and thong. Legs straight, my pelvis rocks forward and back. Quicker. My clit tingles, itches, almost burns from the fabric's rubbing. On my back, knees up, head under the bed. The heel of one hand pressing into my abdomen, two fingers twitching on my g-spot. My spine arches, cunt against the carpet for a moment, and then I crash down. Three fingers now, further in. Nails on my inside ridges. Ripples course through me. Navel, ribcage, nipples, teeth. Faster, faster. My ass on the carpet, back still clothed. Slipping, scraping along the floor. Eyes closed. I can't moan. Sound escapes me, only my fingers inside me. Pressing harder, harder, grasping at the soft place I can feel in my stomach. I remove my fingers, grope for Devin's tower. Still in my pants pocket. Ease the point into me. The chain pressed together with the tip. My other hand on my clit, one finger vibrating. Others on the crease between my lower lips and thigh. Everything moving, every part of me in sync.

Devin, I need you. Where are you?

I rest on the carpet for a while, put my pants on. Leave my thong under the bed, too sensitive right now. The closet, I feel like I should open, so I've explored every part of Devin's room. The doors fold back silently. Hangers, plastic and empty, not even a spare shoe.

No trace of Devin, only a lidded vase on the shelf above my head. Take it down, lid off. Stare inside, just a weird powder. I sneeze. Dip my still-slick fingers in. Pull out. Grey sticks to them, grinds into my fingerprints. Ring finger in my mouth, salty but burnt tasting. Sit on the bed, eyes closed, hugging the vase. Scrape under my nail with my front teeth.

"When I die, you need to feed me to the ocean. None of this keeping me in a jar on display bullshit. I'm not a decoration. I want to travel. I want to see Paris again."

"That'll be a long trip."

"I'll have all the time in the world."

INSIDE

I clomp downstairs.

"How're you doing?" Uncle Roy asks, home now and flipping through TV channels.

"Okay, just packing everything up."

"Your aunt's pretty mad, but I'll miss you. Especially now that you can cook." He grins over his shoulder at me.

"Do you have a plastic bag?" Pause, I need an explanation, "For my toothbrush."

"Yeah, drawer under the cutlery. Can you put on the kettle? I think I'll have some tea."

I nod. "I'll join you in that." Must act natural.

Fill the kettle, boil, make the tea. Give one to Uncle Roy then take mine and a Ziploc bag, and an extra mug for Dacy upstairs.

I leave the mugs on the end table.

The closet is closed, vase not beside the bamboo, where I left it. Panic rises. A pressure behind my ears, throat constricting, pulsating like I need to vomit.

No. I didn't lose her. Not again. I didn't lose Devin, because she isn't in the vase. It must be a dead pet or maybe a grandparent or an elaborate rouse planned by Devin whereby she convinced the mortician to burn only her clothing and put it in the jar to give her family some closure. Anything. Anything else. I can't have lost her again.

Open the closet, empty except the hangers.

"I made tea." I don't quite enter her room.

Dacy ignores me. I sit on the floor, at the seam between hallway carpet and her room. Put the two mugs in front of me. She lies awkwardly on her bed, her ankle wrapped in a tensor bandage and elevated in front of her, an ice bag on top.

Flips her textbook page so it snaps. "Do you think of anyone but yourself?"

"I made you tea."

The vase rests on Dacy's dresser.

"I fucking hate tea!"

Tap my nails against the mugs. Wait.

"Grant won't reply to any of my texts! He thinks I'm some gross incestuous freak because of you! God, if you can't hold your liquor, don't drink so much. And not to mention that I can barely walk! What, am I supposed to hobble to my classes tomorrow?"

"You brought me there. And you bought the shots." I shrug. "Anyway, there's other guys out there. And you just sprained it. Not like it's broken."

"You don't understand! I love him! Have you ever been in love?"

I stand and edge toward the vase. Place the mugs beside it. Reach out to stroke the side. As if touching it would be like holding Devin's hand.

Dacy slams her textbook shut, at least, I think she does. I hear the noise, the heavy thunk, but I can't look at her.

"You're young," I whisper.

"Leave her alone! You already stole my keychain. Are you trying to steal my life, or are you just fucked in the head? You can't have Devin, and you can't preach at me. You aren't my fucking parent or my sister or my cousin. You aren't anything."

"Maybe if you gave one ounce of a shit, you'd know what I'm going through!"

"Because your life is so hard! Goddamn, you're fourteen, things only get worse from here, you're going to need to learn how to deal."

"I'm trying!"

"Smoking pot, and who knows what other drugs, skipping class, graffiti. These aren't signs of dealing. Lighting that boy on fire! What is going through your mind?"

"So ground me, Mom." The way I say it slaps across her face, reminding her she isn't my mother.

"I don't know how to get through to you!" She slams her fist on the counter, downs her wine. "I think you need a change of scenery. I wanted to send you to live with your cousins, but your dad doesn't agree."

"What, tired of putting up with me?" I fidget with my hoodie sleeves. Can't look at her or I'll start crying.

"I'm exhausted."

Dacy didn't come with us to the airport. My uncle stayed home with her too. Her foot bandaged and elevated, still, her head under watch for a concussion. Symptoms can manifest later than the incident. She gets to stay home from school for a week, so no negotiating busy stairwells or buses.

Devin's vase stayed with Dacy, but it's okay. Devin isn't ashes. Aunt Jocelyn guarded me as I got my boarding pass and saw that I made it through security. I could see her standing behind the glass. Glaring at me, lips pressed tight, neck muscle pulsing. No, I could only see that last part in the car ride to the airport. Three hours early for my hour-and-a half flight. She waved at me from behind the sliding doors until I passed the scanning test. No going back. And no smoking after security. I could loop around, sneak out. Stand in line again, remove my shoes, smile, nod, act normal, act normal.

My dad stands on the other side of the metal railing. His smile looks more real than my aunt's, or maybe more concerned. Bethany didn't come with him. Probably didn't want to.

"Suitcase?"

"Nope. Just my bag." I left Dacy's clothes at her house.

No welcome-home hug.

We step outside to the parking lot. Humidity, and the pressing smell of trees. Trees that've been allowed to grow. Leaves unfurled, fat and green against the dark sky. Clouds race over each other, the road below slick from rain. My dad's car's speckled with drops. Smoking's most satisfying when I can breathe this air in afterwards, but I told my dad I quit. I told him and Devin. And I didn't think her funeral was a good place to say I lied. He probably knows, the smell lingering in my clothes, on my hair. But as long as he doesn't see me with a cigarette in my mouth, we can both pretend we believe the lie.

"Do you want to stay the night with me or go to your place?"

"I didn't pay rent." I slide into the passenger seat.

"I called insurance for your car. Your aunt told me what you did to it."

Seatbelt fastened, I stare out the window as he talks.

"It's still under my name. I said I left it, had a business meeting that I couldn't miss." Dad turns on the car and backs out of the stall.

"You don't have business meetings."

"They sent a cheque for your car's value, I put it toward your rent."

"How much?"

"Four grand. I have the leftover money at home."

So, the illusion of space, privacy. But really, I have no choice. I'll have to see him. Go to his house, his domain. No, that's not fair.

My dad loves me, and he's doing what he thinks is best. I should thank him, but I can't squeak out the words.

"We're going to have to talk about this, you know. But not now. I'll let you get settled first."

He looks so tired. Almost as exhausted as Mom sounded all those years ago.

APARTMENT

The place I started looking for Devin. The place I should call home.

In the fridge drawer, a half head of bok choy floats in its own juices, accompanied by two wrinkled oranges. A furry blue-green blanket covers the block of cheddar. At least I still have a jar each of dill pickles and spicy peppers. I take out the cheese, pickles, and peppers. Dinner. Coughing, I leave the rest because it reeks a vinegary-sweet smell that the fridge door blocks. Knife out, hack off the mould, then slice the cheese without rinsing the blade. Cut the pickles with the same knife, leave the peppers whole. Arrange on a plate. Put the kettle on to boil and find my blanket. Naked underneath, the soft folds reassure me. Whisper "hello," and "good to hold you again."

I take my plate to the couch, try a few bites. Salty and slimy and sour, and exactly the same as I remember. But I want curry.

Instead, I make tea. Jasmine bags found in a dusty box in my top cupboard. Eat the rest of my dinner without tasting it and shove the plate across the coffee table. I hold my mug under my nose and inhale, tuck my toes under a couch cushion. Let my book fall open. All this time, and I haven't finished it. And I still can't read. Too quiet. No Dacy, no Uncle Roy, no aunt. No Thea or smells of cooking and memories of absent children. Or sitting down like a proper family and talking about how our days went.

I doze while reading, words swirling, tangling, jostling.

Like legs under sheets. Arachne loves Thomas, no doubt, so maybe Dacy's way isn't so wrong. What about me?

Flare. A cigarette. I clear the words from my eyes, using smoke to make them water. But no tears. Blink, blink. Blink. Near the end. Do I want to finish?

I hold the book open and inhale again. Leave my mouth agape so the tendrils can escape. Wisps like feathers, like wingtips that refuse to choke me. Blowing out, releasing birds across the ink and paper, I see the words again. Arachne disappears, follows my smoke and retreats to the north, leaving her own trail of multi-coloured underwear. If only Devin had left such distinct markers behind her.

Another cigarette. Book closed, on the table, Devin's tower poised on top. I don't know if I sleep or just stare at the keychain for hours. The dark loops into daylight.

Morning, I turn on my phone, check those messages I've been ignoring. Dad's voice increasing in panic, a warbly, barely controlled tone. I delete those messages without listening through. He found me, not that I was lost. And then from Kramer. Angry, pissed that I missed so many shifts. Obviously, I don't have a job. Not that I thought I would.

Might as well visit my dad. Get this talk over with.

I dress in my own clothes. Jeans with creases from being folded in my drawer, and a sweater, because sweaters don't wrinkle. Much.

No need for a jacket. The flowers are already in bloom here. Tulips and fawn lilies, delicate and pink, orange, white. May bursts with colour through the drizzle. The air, wetter, heavier than in Calgary, clings to my skin. Exposed throat, earlobes, knuckles, the damp seeps, seeks. And I find comfort in this closeness, like the air wants to console me. I take out Devin's photo, our photo, at the café. Colours so bright, brighter even than the flowers here in the pots beside the bus stop. Like she never left. And then the bus roars, sloshes grey mud from last night's puddles onto my toes. Door squeals open. No one gets off.

"Hello there, miss! Heading my way?" The driver, grey haired with a wide mouth.

"Apparently," I answer, still looking at my photo. Trying to convince myself she isn't alive, isn't still as vibrant as that day.

I step up, then pause at the coin receptacle. The bus costs money. Shit. I rummage in my pockets, holding Devin with my free hand. A few quarters and nickels between both my pockets, not enough, but I drop it in the slot like it is.

"Hey," the driver touches my sleeve. "That's a nice photo. You should keep it in a frame, somewhere safe so it doesn't get water damaged."

I smile at him. "Will do."

Bethany opens the door, my dad's door. She's barefoot, wearing a fluffy pink housecoat.

"Oh, you. Phil, your daughter's here!" She calls over her shoulder.

From the kitchen: "Morning, sweetheart! I've got eggs and hash browns on the go!"

Bethany doesn't make eye contact as I step inside. Leave my shoes on the mat. Slump to the table as breakfast sizzles.

"How was your visit to Calgary?" Bethany refills her coffee and reaches for a clean mug.

It's like they were expecting me. Like we'd planned to do brunch and catch up after a vacation. Like we're all adults, and no one's concerned for my mental stability, or instability, or whatever they think is going on. Like Devin never existed.

"She'll have iced tea, Beth." Dad folds an omelette without looking up.

I sit cross-legged on the chair, hands in my lap. "Good. I learned how to make curry."

She sits, passes me a glass of iced tea.

"Thanks."

"Your dad tells me your car got stolen while you were out there." Bethany—Beth—raises eyebrows in question as she drinks her coffee with both hands on the mug.

I look at my dad. He whistles, transfers the eggs from the pan onto a plate, then piles the hash browns into a ceramic bowl. Even cubes, but not the kind from a freezer bag. Hand cut. Probably done up last night, then soaked in water to coax the starch from the potatoes. Dried and baked with a drizzle of olive oil. The recipe, the process, comes back to me all at once. As if I've made it myself.

I sip my drink. "Yeah."

"At least insurance came through for you. But it's a pain to deal with, regardless."

"Come dish up." Dad passes us each an empty plate.

I go to the washroom, around the corner and past the stairs. Linger, flipping my hair one way and then the other. Squeeze at a pimple on the corner of my nose. A red blob appears, but nothing pops, nothing oozes. Outside the kitchen, back against the wall. Spurts of running water echo off pans. I don't want to wash dishes. Did enough of that while pretending to be part of Dacy's family.

"Phil—" tap on, tap off, "—your daughter, but I—" tap on, tap off, "—you can't treat her like a baby."

"She doesn't respond to discipline. Her mother and I tried after the incident with the drugs and the fire. Stricter rules fed her bad behaviour, but the group therapy was a good influence. She just—she needs love."

Snort.

I slide down the wall, knees into my chest.

"Devin was good for her. They connected, kept each—" water running "—I wish she were still here."

"I'm sorry, but you need to step up. I can't just eat breakfast with her and pretend everything's okay. She needs to face the consequences."

Tap on again, for longer. I think about leaving, just walking out the door. But. But. Water turns off. Consequences. That ugly word that sounds so much like blame and regret without reason. But still, somehow, consequences are what you deserve, like karma, like the universe has judged you, and there's nothing else to it.

I walk into the kitchen, and I think I'll let it go, pour more iced tea, make small talk until Dad gives me the rest of my insurance money, then fabricate an excuse to leave, but I can't deal with all these people thinking they have a right to my life.

I see her, and the words escape me before I think better of them. "What consequences, Bethany?"

She's drying the pans now. Bathrobe draped over a chair, wearing a lace tank top. Dad leaning on the counter, coffee cup in hand.

Bethany opens her mouth. Closes it.

"Do you mean watching Devin get sicker every day? Seeing her drained and pale and knowing it was all my fault? Do you mean holding the air where her hand should have been? When I left her, and came back, and she was gone, and everyone said she died? What, Bethany? What consequences should I face?"

"I—I'm not your mother."

"No, you're not. My mother died."

Dad stands straighter. Cup down on the counter, an audible clunk. "Out."

I light a cigarette. Elbows over the railing. I could just leave, but I've done that too many times. Maybe Dacy's right, and there's something important about not leaving. About staying. Maybe, eventually, Dad won't want me back. The door behind me opens.

Dad stands beside me. Doesn't reprimand me for smoking. We stare ahead, at the house across the way. A neighbour kneels in her flowerbed.

Dad breaks the silence. "Beth's crying."

"Shouldn't you comfort her?"

"I'm your parent."

The neighbour glances at us, waves with her spade. I knock the ash off the tip, and it falls into Dad's flowerbed below. Rains over the bleeding-hearts and tiger lilies.

I avoid eye contact with the neighbour, but Dad calls across: "Morning!"

"Nice day. Summer's really here!" She responds, wiping her forehead with her arm for emphasis.

"Seems like it."

She gathers her watering can, walks around the side of her house. I keep staring at her flowerbed, half planted. The sun doesn't yet touch us, the front porch shaded by an overhang of roof.

"I want to know you're okay."

I need Devin. "I am okay."

"You haven't acted like this since before Devin." He's leaning with one elbow next to mine, chest facing me.

"Like what?" I can't look at him, so I focus on my lit cigarette. Watch the ash eat the end of the stick. I don't bother to lift it to my mouth. The orange fades, but I roll it between my fingers, unable to drop the cigarette in Dad's garden.

"I thought you were in control. Your mother called. I had to lie. Told her you were too busy at school for a visit."

"She always says she'll come visit, but when was the last time she did?"

"She loves you. You know, I thought you'd reconnect after Devin died. And you didn't, and that was okay, because at least you didn't shut down." He says my name, and I make eye contact, "I can't believe this is all about that picture."

"How can you always move on? Millie, and then Mom who wasn't technically Mom, and now Bethany?" I gulp for air, look up, and blink until I feel the tears receding. "How can you be okay when you're left behind?"

"I always had you. But now I'm not so sure."

"Some days I think it'd be great to just disappear."

"Yeah?"

Devin spreads her arm wide. "I could go anywhere, be anyone. Not that sick girl, not that one-armed weirdo. Well, maybe still that. But I'd be cool—get my stump tattooed, pierce my lip and have a chain connect it to my earring. Pretend I lost my arm in a gang fight, or went crazy and cut it off in the name of art." She grins, all teeth.

"Your mom'd be thrilled."

"But that's the best part. I'd disappear, no one would know."

"Would I?" And a rush, not wanting to hear her answer, "How do you conjugate *être*?"

My homework spread across both our laps in her hospital bed. She told me to keep up my French, even after our trip. Said it would be useful, someday. That we'd have to go back—revisit our favourite spots, and maybe get a little closer to the Eiffel Tower.

If I were more like Devin, I could disappear, too. I've mastered leaving, but she discovered how to disappear. I'd find her, and escape family and rules and the judge-y glares, and adults who still think I'm a kid and tell me what to do. We'd build a home where nothing could touch us. But I'm not like Devin. And now I can't even leave my dad's front step, so maybe I'm not so good at leaving after all.

The neighbour walks back around the front of her house, this time carrying a tray of baby plants. I'm sitting, waiting for Dad to come back with my insurance money. We tried to talk, but there wasn't much to say. He wants me to be a child, dependent on him.

Bethany opens the door and sits next to me. "I'd like to apologize." She's changed out of her robe and now wears jeans and a T-shirt stained with dried paint.

I'm supposed to say, "me too," or "no, I'm sorry," but I can't, and she didn't really apologize, anyway. I bite at a hangnail.

She breathes out. "Look, I'm not trying to be your mom. But your dad and I are moving in together, and so you and I need to get along." Bethany speaks fast, like she's memorized these words from somewhere else and needs to get them out before she forgets.

I raise my head. Her cheeks are puffy, nostrils red. Bethany rubs the back of her hand under her eyes.

She turns away. Aims her attention at the neighbour, who digs, waters, plants, and waters each hole before moving onto the next.

"Okay." I say, "Are you moving in here, or . . . ?"

Bethany nods. "We've been painting, upstairs, the last few weekends." She gestures at her shirt. "Phil's so, so, I don't know. He insisted we paint and make the walls ours before I got settled. Strange, but sweet."

"Mhm," I hum in agreement. He was like that with Devin. Had her share my room until we could paint hers. Like wall colours matter, could somehow have a hand in whether someone stays or goes.

"I don't want you to feel like I'm overstepping or anything," Bethany begins, the airiness of her voice gone now that she's not talking about my dad, "but I called the manager at the Starbucks I used to run and she's willing to interview you for a part-time position. Just to help get you back on your feet."

I take a moment to process. If I don't disappear, I need to work. Pay rent, buy groceries, maybe save for a new car. Or follow Devin, find Devin. No, I can't do that until I get another car, and I don't know where to go next, and I don't think I have it in me to leave again and then come home without her. And sitting here, in the sunshine, on the cusp of summer, it's hard to imagine Devin's still out there. If only I could learn to disappear.

Dad joins us outside before I respond. Likely he was waiting, giving us time to talk, before coming to give me my cash. Probably afraid I'd take the money and run, and he'd never see me again. I stand, and he hands me an envelope. We hug. He draws me in close, tight, like when Devin died. When they said she died. I pull back, cross my arms in front of my chest.

Bethany stands, her hands in her pockets as if unsure if she should also hug me. I smile at her, then wave, and we all say our goodbyes, our compliments about breakfast. Voices a little too high, too light. Pretend we're a normal family.

"Hello, what can I whip up for you today?" Name tag says "George," but the barista looks like a young woman—red cheeks, a Monroe piercing, curly hair pinned back with a shiny headband.

"I'm looking for Priscilla." Warm coffee smells assault me even on the customer side of the counter.

"Just stand by the shelf, I'll grab her for you. *Pris!*" She hollers over her shoulder.

The shelf holds three different types of one-pound coffee bean bags and several travel mugs of varying sizes. I restrain myself from rearranging the display, from hiding the coffee. Luckily, most of the drinks here are only vaguely reminiscent of coffee, so I think I'll be okay to make them. Coins clink against glass.

"Thanks a latte!" George chirps, and I back away from the shelf.

A customer steps around me. Waits at a cut-out in the counter for her drink.

"Hi there, I'm Priscilla." An overweight woman comes out of the back room and starts speaking as she walks over, "Bethany told me to you'd be by. You're Phil's daughter, right?" Younger than I expected. Probably closer to thirty than Bethany's forty-something. Hair tied up, shirt tucked in, and tattoos encircling both wrists.

I reach for her extended hand. "Yes, Dacy, I go by my middle name."

"Nice to meet you. Usually I'd go through the whole interview she-bang and get back to you, but three of my guys called in today, and I could really use you right now. And Bethany's a great woman, she was my manager for years. If she says you're worth a chance, then I trust that."

"Start right now? Really?"

"Yeah, just basic stuff, refilling empty containers, cleaning the workspace. George can handle the till, and I'll do the bar. Might even show you some popular drinks, if you're up for it. We can do the paperwork at the end of the day. But you'll have to fill it out with your full name, for accounting purposes."

I nod in response. She sets me up with an apron, passes me an elastic band to tie back my hair. The result is atrocious, the previously shaved side looking like a mangled mullet with the longest bits hanging around my ear, refusing to go back or lie flat. I should have gotten a haircut. George laughs at me when I come out from the back room.

"Hun, let me help you."

She stands behind me, pulls my hair free. Her nails scrabble at my scalp. Wrenching my hair, twisting. George doesn't take long though, and shows me how it looks in the shiny espresso maker. Now I have a braid from one ear to the other, my long hair flipped over the short chunk.

"There. Now, time to work. Fill the syrups and whipped cream. Wipe down the bar." She points to the ingredient containers and wiggles her hand at the built-in coolers under the counters.

I'm not sure if her gesture means that I should start filling ingredients or cleaning that part of our station. Stainless steel espresso machine atop a peeling counter with metal corner protectors. Cupboards underneath. Cream, drying, though still drip, dripping. Clear and smeared and not dripping at all, just sticky. Pitchers with pink and green and brown melted in the bottoms, measuring scoops scattered. The counter lined with small white and black labels because everything has a place, but nothing's in its place. Except the equipment.

Priscilla dominates one corner, expertly lining up the cups and pressing buttons on the espresso machine as she steams soymilk. She makes two drinks at a time—and I hope she doesn't expect me to do that anytime soon. Finishes them with a crisscross of caramel sauce.

A sink in the corner with a thin blue cloth. I start there, mostly to get out of the way. Wet the cloth, can't find soap, squeeze it damp. Scrub at the cupboards, because I can't stand the sound of the drip pebbling the laminate beneath. I fight with the sticky mess and realize it's hardened on—probably hasn't dripped for hours, but the sound rings in my ears anyway.

Priscilla bustles, accidentally kicks my heel. Coffee hisses and spits. Whipped cream sputters, stutters, and then spills over the edge of the cup onto my clean door.

"Sorry! Can you refill this for me?" She jiggles the canister at me. "Pour some cream in, add eight pumps of vanilla syrup, attach a whip charger, and shake."

I stand, take the offered container, and put everything together. The charger, a thin, vibrator-shaped cannister of carbon dioxide, screws into place. Shake, shake. And then everything explodes. Cream all over me, my apron, shoes, licking my forehead. George doubles over at the till. Laughter trips over itself like ankles in cords.

Curbside, cars wait like leashed dogs for drivers, owners. None of them mine. I take the bus. Everyday, the same meandering route. Nothing like the C-train in Devin's hometown. Direct. Plunging. Or maybe it's not the cars, but the people waiting for buses who are dogs. Expectant and panting.

I hate dogs.

STARBUCKS

"That's one quad-shot half-sweet soy caramel macchiato *sans* caramel drizzle. And an iced, non-fat white mocha with eight pumps raspberry." I pass the drinks through the window after the couple pays, and finish with: "Thank you, and have a grande!"

"Good one!" George high fives me. She doesn't know I've adopted her corny slogans because they're so awful. Part of me hopes a Starbucks higher-up will come for a surprise visit, hear George's annoying puns, and ban them for being off brand. Then again, with my luck, they might make the puns mandatory. Sometimes I really miss working with the dead. The only lame pun I had to put up with was the name of the funeral home, Mourning Glory. Groan. Must be a curse of all workplaces.

No one pulls up to the drive-thru speaker, so I lean against the counter. Draw moustaches on cups where the sleeves will cover them. A bang on my window breaks my concentration, and the Sharpie moustache trails down the length of the cup. I glance over and see a huffy white woman, her fist raised, pounding on my window.

"Excuse me!" The frowning, yoga-clad woman screeches as I open the window.

"Hello?"

"I've been trying to order for the past three minutes. Your machine must be broken."

I glance outside. She stands with one hand on her hip, the other holding a leash attached to a massive German Shepherd. I bite the inside of my lip to keep from laughing, recover, and ask: "Do you have a car?"

"Why do I need a car to get coffee?" Her dog barks his opinion.

"The weight of the car is what turns on the machine."

"What does that matter?"

Exasperated, I roll my eyes and explain, "The drive-thru is for people with cars."

"Can you or can you not get me my coffee?" She slaps her hand on my counter.

"No. You don't have a car. How about you park your dog and come into the café?"

In the background, George laughs and rolls her eyes. She heard the whole exchange over our headsets. I lob my graffitied cup at her head—she catches it and throws it back at me. I guess working with the living isn't so bad.

APARTMENT

My dad wants weekly family dinners. To make sure I'm all better, or at least okay. I should tell him I can't stand coffee or cranky people who haven't had their coffee yet, or people who have no common sense and refuse to understand the basics of drive-thrus.

Jeans and a blouse—look the part first. Then try.

Except I can't go to dinner and sit and talk and pretend like I did at Dacy's. Family. Family keeps tying me to one place, refuses to let me find Devin. Insists on painting over her existence. I saw last week, after dinner, I used the upstairs washroom and I saw they'd painted Devin's old room, my mom's old room. Thought Bethany meant they were painting the master bedroom before she moved in, and maybe they did, but now the other Mom's/Devin's space is hospital-room beige, and so is my old room. Plain. Painted over for a fresh start without absent mothers or dead nieces or problem daughters.

I call him and say I'm not feeling well, that I probably caught a cold from a customer, even in the summer heat. And I do feel sick, or something. Unwell. I bundle myself under the covers on my bed, and wait and wait, and wish that Devin could come back. To me. But I sense she won't, and how can I find her when she's vanished?

STARBUCKS

An old lady, crumpled over her walker, hobbles to the counter. I've seen her before. Every few days she's in with a woman in her late fifties. Mother and daughter alike will go off on whoever's working till. The old lady always asks for "the foam stuff."

I'm officially certified as a barista, meaning I can make coffee unsupervised and usually manage to avoid exploding anything. I think she wants a dry cappuccino.

Today the old lady is alone. She waits at the front, skin around her eyes pulling down, mouth parted enough to show the coral lipstick on her front teeth.

The girls on till ignore her, except Trish, who cups a hand around her ear and leans over the counter.

"I can't hear you!" As if the old lady is deaf.

"The foam! The one with foam, you stupid girl. Is there anyone around here who knows how to make coffee?"

Trish rolls her eyes, and George and the other girls giggle as she says, "Dacy, you're up." I jolt, momentarily forget my name, and look for Dacy. They laugh as if I'm in on a joke—like I'm pretending to look for myself or that I'm pretending to be someone other than myself. I'm not sure which.

I look at the lady as I approach. Thick, grey white hair set by rollers, a floral T-shirt exposing flabby triceps like limp wings.

"Hi, what can I get for you today?" I smile, maybe too big.

"You're going to make me repeat myself again? Idiot girl. I asked you to find someone who can get me the foam stuff."

"Okay, so a dry cappuccino? What size?"

"No, none of this fancy shit. A small mug of the foam."

I nod, make sure my smile is fixed in place. "Okay, I'll get that for you. Want to find a seat and I'll bring it to you?"

"Wait, wait, I have to pay first." She holds out a handful of loose change. Mostly nickels and pennies, but a loonie too. "Is this enough?"

I've already rung her order through as one of my free drinks for the day.

"Yes, that's perfect." I take her dollar and forty-three cents and deposit it in the tip jar after she's turned away.

Everyone's fled to the backroom, except George, who's on drive, so I go to make the drink.

Push the button, pour the shot into the mug. I give her one of our ceramic to-stay mugs because she likes to sit on the patio with her drink. Steam the milk into the shot six seconds after the espresso. Any longer than ten and the shot goes dead. Tastes burnt, like coffee left in a pot too long and made without a filter so the grounds get stuck in your molars. I had to drink dead shots as part of my training, had to learn never to serve them. Though, in my opinion, not dead shots are hardly better.

When the cappuccino is done, most of the cup is filled with foam and light to pick up. I wish I could make a fancy design on the top for her, a leaf or heart, like I've seen George and Pris make, but I'm not that good.

Instead of setting the mug on the counter and hollering out the order, I walk it out the door and to the old lady in her usual spot on the patio.

"Here you are, one mug of the foam."

She looks at me, eyes wide and a bit watery, like she can't control her body anymore. Both hands on the mug she takes a sip. I go to turn away, but she stops me.

"What's your name?"

"Dacy." I point to my nametag on my apron.

"Dacy." She repeats, foam caught on her upper lip hair. "Thank you. I'm Gwen. This is perfect. I'm going to ask for you next time; the other girls think I'm dumb or losing my mind, but you actually understand me."

I move to leave again, to go back behind inside and the counter. Gwen extends her fingers and touches my hand.

"Will you sit with me? I've no one today."

"Where's your daughter?"

"Daughter? She left years ago. Called me a miserable witch because I didn't like her fiancé."

"But the woman who comes in with you?" I sit across the table from her, because she grips my wrist. The chair warm from the sun.

"Her, I pay her to be with me. I'm in the home just down the street. It's Linda's day off."

"Oh."

"She takes care of me, but she can be downright nasty. Always talking over me, *clarifying*, she says. Like people don't understand what I say. But you do." She releases my wrist and pats my hand.

Gwen takes another sip. I should get back to making drinks, but then this little old lady would be alone.

"Dacy, you're a sweet girl. You wouldn't disappoint your mother and abandon her."

"She left me. And so did Devin."

"Doesn't matter who left. You must find them, because whatever you did, it won't justify your loneliness. I was too damn stubborn to know that earlier. Now, I'm too old."

I hum in agreement, and watch the cars coming and going in the parking lot. Our patio setup isn't the best—a few tables, each with chairs for two, outside our front door. People walking by often step into the parking lot to pass this busy section.

Gwen finishes her foam drink in silence, and stands, patting me on the shoulder with one hand, the other still clutching the ceramic mug. I let her walk away with it.

Back inside, I expect to catch shit for sitting in the sunshine, but I'm prepared to argue I went for a break, even though mine technically isn't scheduled for another hour.

Instead, George remarks, "I've never seen her so pleasant."

I grab a cloth and start wiping the counter.

"Did you tell Dacy what the old hag wanted?" Trish, hands on her hips.

"You knew what she was asking for?" I bristle.

"Everyone does," Trish scoops ice into the blender. "She's in here all the time."

"Then why didn't you take her order?" I shout over the noise, as Trish makes a green tea frap.

George answers for her, "She's a bitch. Calls us stupid every time she's in here. You get what you give."

"She's lonely." I rub at a spot of syrup stuck on the counter.

Trish turns off the blender and pours the drink into a plastic cup. "Doesn't mean she can yell at me." She swirls a whipped cream tower over the drink.

"Have you ever tried to be nice?" Stand up, my hands on the counter, and I feel I must look like Aunt Jocelyn when she was trying to be patient with me.

"Why?" Trish slides the drink over the counter and calls out the customer's name.

I throw my cloth in the bucket of sanitizer. Untie my apron and toss it in the bin with the other dirty ones, my nametag with my borrowed name still attached. Take my tote bag from the backroom. I was wrong earlier. Working with the living is far worse than with corpses. Leave.

BUS STOP

Trapped, without a car. Shackled to the bus schedule, the same roads. Every day. Get ready early, and stand at the stop until the bus roars up. The same driver in the morning, always quiet. Perpetual travel mug that could have coffee or tea or something stronger. And the evening driver, chatty, but only with the regular passengers. He's older, probably retired, then got bored of being at home with his wife, so now he drives young professionals, and students, and the woman who always has grocery bags. Talks to them like he cares, like he's interested. Maybe he is, but only in the banal details: "How's work going?" and "Did your classes go well this semester?" He never asks about Devin. Didn't recognize her when I showed him my pictures. Then again, why would she take the bus?

Every day, I hope it'll be a different bus driver. Maybe even Arachne, called into being from the book pages. Surly expression, dark hair, ready to flee. But it won't be. These fictions I believe in swirl behind my closed eyes until I can't believe that Arachne doesn't drive. She must. Except that she escaped into the cold. The north. Not a place where Devin could survive. She needs a humming city, and people to marvel at her flashing colours.

I can't wait for this bus any longer. Not today. I need to run, escape. Drive. I don't have a car.

APARTMENT

I pack my large purse, the one that has a long and a short strap, with a change of clothes, *No Fixed Address*, even though I'm finished, Devin's tower, and my photo of us. Passport. Check the expiry date, still good, for one more year. In the bathroom, I lob off the long half of my hair to match the other side. Cut chunky bangs. Not Dacy or Lainey or Robin or Pigeon or Rachelle or Arachne. Someone else. Maybe someone closer to myself.

I don't bother locking my door. Walk, shaking my head. Feel the lightness. Cars and streets with older buildings made of concrete blocks. End up at the marina, Empress Hotel behind me, and I wonder who they hired to replace Rachelle's grandma. I walk down the concrete stairs. Closer to the water. Stands set up near the boats. Artwork and trinkets, and not that different from Paris. I sit on the edge, my arms looped over the large chain strung up to keep people safe. Another chain above my head. Pull out a cigarette and take off my shoes. On my back, I could slip down the ledge, into water more green than blue. Fall under a yacht, deeper and deeper. But I don't. I keep sitting with my legs over the edge, the water too low for my feet to reach. Blowing smoke over the clouds. People walk around me, don't glance down. I flick the stub at the water, watch the ripples.

Circular, outward. Looping like time. And disappearing, always in the middle of a disappearing act.

Eventually, I stand. Eventually, I walk away.

Doors slide apart. Waiting room. Plastic chairs, grey and white tiles, and a desk, the kind with a raised counter and a pen tied to a string taped on top. No one in line. Six people in the chairs, shivering, coughing. Some looking fine except for bruises under their eyes.

"How can I help you?" Bright headband behind the counter.

I tuck my hair behind my ear. "I'm here to see my cousin. She's in ICU."

"Name?"

"Devin Evans."

She types, glances at the screen. Frowns. Computers and telephones beep around us. People cough, sneeze. A kid laughs and is shushed.

"We don't have a patient in ICU by that name. Are you sure she isn't at the Jubilee?"

"I just visited her."

"Any chance you can sneak me Jell-O next time you come? All they give me is vanilla pudding."

I know Devin doesn't mean the pre-packaged Jell-O. She wants me to use the powdered stuff that comes in a box and mix in fresh fruit while it sets overnight.

"Green apple, with raspberries?" I confirm, just so she knows I already know.

Devin smiles. "And blackberries from that bush." The one that spills out of someone's yard, branches thrust through the fence, berries suspended over the sidewalk.

She squeezes my hand. Her other arm under the blanket so my aunt, who just sits across the room, reading Harlequin paperbacks, doesn't freak out. We can't talk like we used to. Supervised by parents and nurses. No hope of midnight escapades when Devin needs constant monitoring. They, everyone, say "fear of relapse," like she's in rehab for too many drugs—her mother's greatest fear.

One hand, shrivelled and black, had to be cut off already. Fear of having to take the forearm, then the rest. How much of her will they chop off?

I stub my cigarette and walk back inside. The same headband in scrubs mans the desk. Eyes on her screen. I sit in a plastic chair. Flip open my book. Arachne's follower knows her story's not over yet. But I know the end.

The receptionist turns through the door behind her, an office, probably. I stand, walk around the corner, find the elevators. Up, up, up. Put my book in my purse, sling the strap across my body. Turn right, then press the intercom button because the door's locked.

"Hello."

"I'm here to see the patient in ICU bed seven."

"One moment please." The intercom disconnects, and a few seconds later the doors swing wide.

Through another hallway and more doors, then left past the nurses' station and keep going. The ICU is just one large room, beds separated by curtains and arranged in a circle. Each bed has a number on the wall above it. One nurse for every two patients. I slip beside Devin's bed, but there's someone else in it.

An old man, wrinkled into his sheets, hand on the remote, but eyes on the window. Cords from his mouth, elbows, and hands lead to bags on stands. Some bulge, some almost flat, different clear liquids. Devin had the same, for a while. The cords seem to trap him. A fly caught in a web, cocooned in too many blankets and left to be deflated.

He hasn't seen me, hasn't moved. And I want him to get away, be free. Run like Devin did. I step closer, closer. Pull the cord closest to me. Yank it from the vein leading to a finger. The needle tip emerges, long. Yellowish, like a spider fang dripping venom. Alarms sound, the old man screams, but this happened when the cord came free. And I stand there holding it, looking at the end, not at the blood and torn skin on the old man's hand matching the skin on the cord, held in place by a thick band of tape. Thrashing, his cords wind tighter. Ringing, buzzing, beeping from monitors. An incessant keen, laced with spittle from his small mouth.

Two hands take my forearms. Another pinches the tube from my grasp. White coats flurry between myself and the old man.

"No! No, no, no, no, no! Let him go!"

I don't know if anyone replies, or if they just talk around me. The hands behind me push, shove. My heels can't find purchase, but my toe catches on the tile. Knees buckle, I pitch forward, shins into the ground. I try to scramble under the curtain, to the next bed. Can't. Hauled up. Two people, one on each arm, march me to the nurses' station. Inside the office behind the desk. Just a doorway, no door, filing cabinets, more plastic chairs and a table.

"What's your name?" One of my captors.

No one sitting at the outside desk.

"What are you doing here?" The other white coat.

A man comes into the station, picks up the phone, "We have a woman here . . ."

"Are you on medication?"

". . . don't think she's a patient . . ."

"How long have you been off your medication?"

". . . thanks. We'll keep her at the fourth-floor station . . ."

"If you don't talk to us, we can't help you."

I continue staring at the plain wall. Taupe. Devin says taupe is a soothing colour. I disagree.

They can't hold me here, tie me down in their webs. Force pills through my teeth. I don't need fixing. I hug my purse, surprised they didn't try to take it, to see if I have pills already in it. That's what the police will do, once they get here. And I'm sure they're on their way. ID and drug check. I know the drill.

Two of the coats leave. The last takes a chair across the room from me. Perpendicular. Rifles through a sheaf of paper and clicks a pen.

"We just want to help." She buries her head in work.

Nothing moves in the hallway. A beep comes from the computer, and the nurse goes to investigate. My prison has a window. All the nurses crowd around the old man.

My one chance. Through the doorframe, around the corner. Someone, one of my captors, shouts. Devin and I used to explore, wander these halls. Footsteps slap behind me. There's a staircase on either end of each floor with doors that open without permission. I whip through a stairwell, down, down. Hear a door slam above me. Across the second floor, easy to pass through nurses and patients, pretend to be someone's family. Down the opposite stairs. Weave around the first floor, into the emergency room. Blood and crying and someone screaming and coats and stethoscopes flailing. I exit the emergency doors. The PA system calls out, "Code green on the east stairs."

Wailing, I force myself to cry. Let tears pool over my cheeks so my pain is obvious. Real.

"Are you okay?" A nurse takes my shoulders.

"My . . . my . . . sister! I, I can't watch anymore!"

"Do you need to sit down?" Her face a practiced concern.

"Fre . . . fresh air."

"Okay, let me walk you outside. There's a bench."

"Thank. Thank you."

She rubs my upper arm. Comforting. Near the door, a woman sleeps curled over her legs. I trip on her open bag, spill the insides. Palms into the ground. The women jerks awake, stuffs her things, wallet and receipts, back into her purse, slides her bag under her chair. Doesn't speak.

"Here, let me help you." The nurse takes me by the waist and deposits me on the bench. "If you need anything, just come get me. My name's Carrie."

I wrap my arms around my stomach. "Okay. Thanks."

She pats my shoulder and goes inside. I keep curled up, rocking forward and back, in case Carrie glances at me. From the bench I hit the unlock button on the car keys. Taillights flash on a blue Honda Civic a few rows away. I took a chance, tripping over the bag, and it worked better than I expected. Now, I can drive. Check through the glass doors. Can't see Carrie, but the other nurse is talking to one of my captors. I walk to the car, not too fast, my purse bumping along my hip.

Slip into the driver's seat. This is where I belong. Turn the key. Dashboard icons light, engine doesn't roll over. Gear shift, three pedals. Standard.

Devin in the driver's, Dad beside her, and me in the back.
"Why won't it turn on?"
"Put your foot on the clutch."
She looks at him.
"The far left pedal. Push it all the way down."
Devin stalled six times from the driveway to the main road. Then my dad took over and drove us to a parking lot. He said learning standard was important so if we ever found ourselves in a bad situation, we could get home. Because what if we were out with someone who drove stick, and they drank too much? And Devin and I laughed and vowed to date only people with automatics. I stalled eight times in one loop of the lot.

IN REVERSE

"Who knew Dad would be right?" I glance to the passenger seat. To Devin.

"Clutch in, turn key, put it in first."

I do, but release the clutch too soon. Stall half out of the parking spot. Through the glass entrance, I see the front desk, people in chairs. No one coming after me. Yet.

"Slower," Devin coaches.

Go through the steps again, careful as Devin directs me. Drive to the exit. Stall at the stop sign. Back in neutral, try again. Get onto the highway, accelerate through the gears to fifth. Doing ninety in the eighty zone. Feeling of driving, really driving. Why couldn't I get this when we practised? I glance to Devin, conspiratorial grin ready, but she's gone. Eyes back on the road.

SIDNEY MAIN STREET

I park on the street, don't pay. Not coming back. Not to consequences or medications or mandatory therapy. Purse in hand, I wander toward the fishing dock, where the natives bring in crab, and small boats take weekend warriors on adventures. Briny but fresh. Squawking seagulls. I toss the car keys into the ocean. They splash and a gull swoops, hoping for a fish.

A restaurant on the corner with a patio. I enter, all the outside tables full, I sit at the bar. A sign on the wall advertises a seventies-themed party tonight at the community centre. The bartender chops limes, and barely glances at me. Her blade quick, precise.

I should order a drink, should appear normal. Maybe that's the key to disappearing—hiding between strangers. Isn't that what Devin said her strategy would be? But what do normal people order? Not rum and coke or cheap beer or vodka cran or blue shots. Then again, I have been Dacy since I've been home, and her drink order is tame, if a little Calgary-specific.

"Hey, any chance you could make me a double Caesar?" I smile at the bartender, "And do you know if anyone around here is heading to the ferry?"

"Um. I think that couple over there mentioned they're taking the seven o'clock." She gestures towards a middle-aged man and woman. A briefcase leans on his chair legs, her long hair in a ponytail.

"Thanks."

I stand, almost walk to them. But the TV above the bar has my face on it. Blurry, grainy, from the hospital security camera. *WOMAN WANTED IN CONNECTION TO VIOLENT ATTACK ON ELDERLY PATIENT AT VICTORIA GENERAL: contact police with tips on whereabouts.* Volume muted, but the words so big they feel like fingers pointing right at me.

Leave, again. Always.

A second-hand boutique rests just off the main stretch. They don't have a TV on their wall. Music plays, uninterrupted by commercials. No radio. The front racks have more traditional clothes. Dress pants, blazers, button-down blouses. I can't pull off that look with my hair in ragged chunks. At the back are furred vests, skirts and shirts tie-dyed and polka dotted.

"Need a hand finding anything, dear?" Grey-haired shopkeeper. Mauve lipstick bleeds into the creases around her mouth.

"Yeah." I close my eyes, try to remember the sign I saw. "Well, I'm going to the community centre party tonight, and my friend said she'd bring me a costume, but now she's not coming . . ." I trail off before I say something that'll give me away.

"Oh, you're going to the seventies-themed fun-money casino! Val, she works here, she organized it this year. Let's see what we can do for you. I don't think I have anything vintage seventies, but we can fake it." She winks at me. "It's great, young people like you coming out to support our local seniors' residence."

She hums, and I flick through hangers. Different textures, colours. I slide my fingers over the fabrics, drawn in by the softest materials. Velour. A chunky knit. Not paying attention to the article of clothing, its cut or size.

"You're what, a six or an eight?"

"Something like that." I look down at myself, I was a two when I knew Devin. But then my hips came in. Will she even recognize me?

"Try these."

She passes me a pair of white corduroy bell bottoms. I peruse the rack of scarves, seeking the silkiest.

"And how about this?"

The woman holds up a tasselled vest and translucent paisley blouse. I nod.

"The change room is just through here." She presses the hangers into my hands. "Show me when you're dressed."

I come out in bare feet. The shirt's a little tight, the pants long.

"Just a few tweaks, and I think you'll be set for your party."

She steps close. Her head below my nose, rose perfume. Nimble fingers unbutton the bottom half of the shirt, then knot it above my navel. Takes a step back, arms crossed.

"And this, and this."

A pair of hoop earrings. Bright orange scarf she arranges over my hair. "You look wonderful!"

Turn to face the mirror. Outrageous. No one would wear this, especially someone trying to hide from police. Devin, is this how you've been hiding? Maybe the best disguise isn't blending in, but standing out in a way no one expects. Being too obvious. A disappearing act in reverse.

"Perfect. I don't know what I would've done without your help."

"No worries, dear. I get bored here, sometimes. Working all alone."

"How much do I owe you?"

She mutters to herself, points to each item. "Let's say eighty dollars and then ten percent friend's discount because you're going to the charity event."

Disguised, I'll get to the ferry, get back to the mainland. That must be where Devin went. She was right there, in the car, with me.

I have a few grand from my car tucked safely in my purse. Enough to pay for a taxi and a ferry and for whatever else I'll need to get to Devin. There's a phone booth near where I parked. Should've saved the keys, but the license plate has probably been reported already. Thank you, Sidney, for being small and old fashioned. Yellow pages inside. Call a cab.

Devin, where are you? My thoughts are too fast, I can barely keep up, and you've run ahead, too. Please wait. Wait for me.

Water sloshes against the ferry as it chugs forward. I spend the journey on the smokers' deck. Inside is too quiet, only the clink of dishes as busboys retrieve dirty plates from empty tables. A low rumble of voices. The occasional shriek from a small child. Out here, conversations ebb as the ocean, wind filling silences. People don't mind so much when you eavesdrop and then join in. I like talking to lonely people. The ones with elbows draped over the rail, eyes on the horizon.

"Sailing solo? I like your jacket."

Purple leather turns to me, "Not sailing alone when there's two thousand or so other people on board too."

"Just because you're in the same place doesn't mean you're together." I reach up to toss my hair, and find the headscarf instead. I twirl the fabric around my finger.

"Are you one of those new-age hippie types?"

"Do you think I am?" I lean on the railing with one elbow, my other arm crossed in front of my body. Squish my tits together. Unintentionally, of course.

He looks at the sea. "You know yourself better than I do."

"In theory." Toss my butt overboard.

Purple leather turns to me, "There's an ashtray right behind you." But he glances down my shirt.

"Where you going tonight?" I light another.

"Home."

"Want some company for the drive? We can get to know each other," I pause dramatically to suck on my cigarette, "a little bit better."

"I prefer to be alone."

No luck. My tits can't compensate for the outfit being too much. That's okay. I'll get a free ride. One way or another.

I sneak onto the parking docks. Technically, they're off limits during travel, but only so people don't keep their cars on and gas the place. I look at the vehicles at the front of the queue, search for a real trunk. Not the kind with the rear-view window built into the trunk. Then search for a half-open window. No point breaking the seal of a closed window with so many options around.

Found the car. Older model, less chance of alarms, backseat window unrolled completely. Reach through the back window and twist my arm around the front seat to hit the unlock button. Retrieve my arm and go to the driver side, pop the trunk. Not too much shit in the trunk, enough room. Too old or too broken, though—no emergency release latch in the trunk. Try another car. Trunk of the next is full, same with the third. But I need a ride, I can't take public transit. Not with my face on the news.

The captain calls over the intercom that we will arrive in twenty minutes. Last chance before people get herded back to their cars. And I find it. A red Honda Accord, pillows and lawn chairs in the trunk, emergency latch, and the backseat console has a removable back, so I won't suffocate. I fold myself in, wedge the pillow under my head, legs over the chairs, knees bent sideways. Not ideal, but I can manage. My right arm is scratched from manoeuvring through various windows and around seatbelts, but not so much that it bleeds. Just raised red streaks.

Thuds and thumps and a mass of voices cascade over the cars minutes after I get settled. A family enters my car. Mom, dad, and teenaged kid, from the sound of them. No, two teens. Voices muffled. Maybe it's a carful of teens, not a family. My hip starts to ache. The car rumbles forward, I lurch with it.

A ringing noise, a finger circling a crystal water glass. But heavier, denser, more like waves against the back of my skull. I can't hear any voices. Breathe slow, even. I want Devin here. Try to summon her back.

Remember when I first told her why I was arrested. Well, sort of arrested. Walking on the beach in January. Long shadows, and our footprints squishing the sand down, pooling with muddy sea. She tucked her hair behind one ear. The breeze pulled it out. I can't remember what we said, how she laughed. I flailed my arms and mimicked the guy who stepped in the fire. Or did the fire spread from him to the grass? I don't remember which version I told her. All I know is that she laughed when I told her, but how did she laugh? Did she howl, face to the clouds? Or muffle her smile with a sleeved hand? I don't know, and she doesn't appear to remind me.

The car hits a few bumps. My forehead into the low trunk lid, then hip into the floor. Knees bang together and against the lawn-chair legs. Hard metal poles. I grit my teeth, jaw locks. The passengers play music, loud, some top-forties pop, I assume. They sing along, but the synthesized lyrics remain indecipherable. My neck aches, along with my hip. The ringing pressure starts to fade. I close my eyes, and I'm back on the ferry, ship rocking beneath me. But the trunk's too cramped, too stale. No wind to whip my skin.

And the car stops. Doors open, slam shut. One, two, three, I breathe deep, six, seven. Roll my shoulders as best I can, flip onto my back. Twelve, thirteen. Nothing stirs in the car, no music, no doors have reopened. Eighteen, nineteen, twenty. Must be safe. I find the latch with my hand. Yank down and the trunk unlocks. Springs up a few centimetres, allows a draft. I gulp. Push the trunk all the way open with a foot, swing both legs over the edge. Try to stand. My legs don't work—they feel like I just came, thin and shaky. I fall out of the car. Elbow hits pavement first, gets skinned, rips the paisley blouse. A blot of blood.

"Dad!" A little girl, seven or eight, her head out the car window, staring at me.

I blink, her father and a teen a few metres away at a hotdog stand. Can't get up.

"What the hell are you doing?" A few passersby stare.

My elbow drips blood on the white pants. The boy rushes up and pulls his sister out of the car with one hand, the other holds two hotdogs.

"Who is she?" Points at me.

The father advances. He's large, three of me wide, thighs in board shorts jiggling like curdled milk in garbage bags. Walks evenly, doesn't draw more attention, doesn't shout.

"That would be a trunk monkey. Nasty creatures, they wear bright colours and hide in trunks trying to scare people like you!"

The brother, he takes the girl's hand, walks her down the street. He keeps her close and doesn't let her turn around to see me again.

Gruff hand on my collar lifts me, shoves my back into the car. Mustard on his chin.

"You like hiding out in other people's cars? Think it's a laugh? Or were you planning on stealing our things?" His stomach presses me closer to the car. People just walk past. "I think the police would like to know about this incident. You good-for-nothing hippie types always sponging off hard-working citizens."

"*Help*! Someone help me!" Hand slams over my mouth, too firm to bite.

I thrash my hands, smack his car. Squirm, crunch his feet under mine. Two men grab my assailant by the shoulders, drag him back. He doesn't fight. I run, my bag, still strapped across my body, swings, hits my already sore hip again and again until I stop.

Merge with a group crossing the street. Look back for a moment, see the two kids walking back toward their car.

I meander the streets, find a bar. Bouncer at the door asks for my ID. Stamps my wrist with a black smudge. The upper floor has organized tables, people in suits and loosened ties. Waitresses in tight T-shirts. Downstairs, a girl asks for ten dollars, there's a show. I get another stamp. Most of the room is a dance floor, sparse tables against the wall, bar in the middle. A country band on a slightly raised stage. They're playing a cover of a radio song, one that Starbucks played every day. I find myself singing along, though they play at a different rhythm than the original.

Go to the bathroom. See how tattered I am in the silty light.

Turn to the girl applying lipstick beside me. "Do you have scissors?" I don't mistake her for Devin. Not even for a moment.

She purses her lips, dabs with paper towel. "Hmm." Digs through her small bag, the insides spill onto the counter and I don't know how she managed to make everything fit inside in the first place. Wallet, earbuds, phone, at least six lipsticks, toothbrush, full-sized bottle of perfume, Clearasil wipes, and a pack of pencil crayons. "No scissors. Only a nail file." She answers, holding it aloft.

"That could work, thanks."

I take off my shirt, pierce the seam for one sleeve. Rip through it. Then the other. Pass the nail file back to the girl. She gathers her items into her purse and leaves.

Shirt back on, now a tank top, sort of. Frayed, but better than the torn elbow. I retie the bottom into a knot above my bellybutton. Use my headscarf as a belt, like I saw at Keelie's houseparty. Back on the dance floor.

I think about going to the bar, ordering the cheapest beer, but one sits abandoned on a table near me. No one around. Half full—I swig the rest in one gulp. People dance, sway, mouth the words with the band. They don't play anything original.

See another beer all alone. I spider it as well. Dance with the crowd to the other side, casually commandeering more warm beers from along the bar and other tables.

"Having fun?" A voice like Devin's climbs the back of my neck.

"Sure." I smile, sure that she's finally let me catch up to her.

"That was my beer."

I finish it. "Huh, sorry."

She laughs, and I turn to look at her, see her purple-ringed lips widen. The bathroom girl. My stomach clenches, and I bite my tongue. Taste her warm beer still coating my mouth. Can't swallow.

"I'm Mallory—you're strange."

The band finishes to applause. I try to ignore Mallory, but she hasn't left my side—keeps smiling at me and attempting small talk. I want to walk away, either forget about Devin entirely in a haze of inebriants or chase her to the end of the world. Can't decide which. But if news of the hospital, the old man, has travelled to the mainland, then being around people will help my disguise. Help me avoid consequence or retribution. A stereo replaces the music while the band members take down. Mallory gestures with two fingers to her lips.

I could go for a smoke. "Why not?"

We head outside in a surge of people as most of the downstairs bar exits.

"Hey, Mal, where'd you pick up the hippie?" A guy nods to me.

"Brydan, this is—what's your name?"

"Val—" I linger on the *l* as I light my cigarette, trying to remember the last half of that name, "—erie."

Mallory throws her arm around me and giggles. The beer and cigarette make my head light and fuzzy. I don't mind the pressure of her arm over my shoulders. Almost like a hug.

"Well, girls, you feel like sticking around? Aaron's throwing a party tonight we could hit."

Mallory releases me and stretches. "I'm down, you?"

Devin, should I try to forget you?

We arrive at the house. An ordinary, upper middle-class suburban house, no music to be heard from the street. Not like Keelie's house. No posters on the door or painted rocks.

"This is it?"

"Yeah. Aaron's 'rents are away for the week. He keeps it lowkey, so his neighbours don't notice."

Inside, music plays from a stereo. People mill with beer cans and plastic cups. The air buzzes, but nothing else. No thuds or gyrating, just listing bodies and chatter. The kitchen table hosts platters of picked-over food. Sliced baguette gone hard from sitting out, empty dip containers, and chip crumbs.

Brydan gets caught in conversation with a guy carrying a box of beer. Mallory and I settle in a corner. People eye me. Discreetly. While talking, they gesture with a chin jut, a pointed glance, or a vague hand wave to barely conceal that they're pointing at me. Others turn, look from my corduroy pants up, then back to their conversations. The stifling politeness of prep-school white people, familiar from my funeral parlour days. I thought a party in Vancouver would be different, that maybe people would be talking about foreign policy or the environmental impacts of transatlantic shipping or any of the other topics covered in university. Like Keelie's party, but better informed. Not just an excuse to gossip about the new girl.

"I'm going to grab us some drinks." Mallory leaves.

Everyone seems so mellow. Is this a party? The room has glass ornaments, vases and paper weights on end tables, the mantel. Under-stuffed chairs people perch on, hardwood floor and beige walls.

"Hi, do I know you?" Freckles, combed hair, shirt tucked in. He looks like a boy, not a host.

"Aaron?"

"And you are?"

"This is Valerie, she came with us." Mallory returns, no drinks.

"Okay. Just so you know, any consumption is to be done off property, preferably across the street."

Mallory rolls her eyes, arms crossed over her chest. "I know the drill."

"Make sure she does." Aaron pinches his lips and walks away. Turns the music even lower.

"He's a prat, but you can always find a dealer at his parties."

I haven't touched hard drugs since Devin. Been too afraid I'd lose myself. Might've happened anyway.

"And they're out of beer already. Want to do a liquor-store run?"

"Yeah, let's do it." Anything to get out of this house.

We pass a couple standing near the door, coats on. The air is always damp, clinging, so close to the coast, even when it's June.

"Need beer?" Mallory asks the tall guy.

He pats his pocket, probably checking for his wallet. "Just heading out. You coming?"

"Definitely. Think you could hook us up too?"

The person standing next to him giggles. Tall guy in studded leather slaps a hand over their mouth.

"You know the rules, Emery."

Emery gasps. "Sorry. Sorry. Everything's just so funny!" The voice low, but wispy, and I can't tell if Emery's a guy or a girl.

I open the door. "Let's go."

We spill onto the sidewalk. Mallory reapplies her purple lipstick as Emery and the leather-wearer named Chris debate which liquor store. The one that's closer or the one with cheaper prices. Androgynous Emery wears high-waisted jeans and a single feathered earring. And me. Disguised as a hippie in 2014. A mullet-esque haircut that wishes it could be a pixie cut. They decide on the closer store, and I don't mind, I have cash, but I'm playing it off like I don't. These are rich kids, or at least they go to rich kid parties. They're already too drunk to really care about who pays for what, and my slight buzz wore off the moment we walked into that oppressive house.

Cross the intersection to a row of Chinese, Thai, Indian, and Sushi restaurants—all of Asia conveniently conglomerated into one block. On the next street, a set of twenty-four-hour drive-thrus, pharmacies, and a liquor store. Chris and Mallory get beer. I light another smoke and lean against the wall with Emery. A few minutes later, Mallory and Chris emerge with a case of Pabst.

Mallory passes me a beer, hers already open. "Cheers!"

Liquid sloshes over the edge, over her fingers. Emery doubles over again.

"Here you are." Chris produces two white squares.

Smaller than my pinkie nail, and thinner too.

"Put it on your tongue." Mallory instructs. "Let it just soak in." As if I don't know how to drop acid.

We each finish a beer in the parking lot. Leave the cans in a row. Decide not to go back to Aaron's. Decide we want food. Lug the case of beer to the nearest drive-thru. A sign on the intercom says: "Car required." Should've had that at Starbucks, but it doesn't stop us now. Position ourselves in an invisible car. Jump at the same time on the sensor. Nothing. Drive to the window. Mallory knocks, a middle-aged man opens the window a crack.

"Hello, good sir. It appears your ordering sign is out of service. Can we get four burgers, four chocolate milkshakes, and a shit-ton of fries?"

Her hands don't leave the steering wheel. We all squat in our invisible seats.

"Can't you kids read?"

"Yes, but what does that have to do with fries?"

"No car. No service." The drive-thru attendant slams the window closed and walks out of sight.

"The fuck? Twenty-four hours my ass." Emery shouts.

We stomp away with our beer. Sit in the middle of the parking lot and drink another each. Soon I'm laughing, and Mallory's laughing, and so is everyone, and the drive-thru guy becomes hilarious. We take turns impersonating him. Forget our hunger.

I look up. Try to see stars, but the city lights are in the way. The moon has an orange shadow. It pulsates, then sparks. The edges of buildings flash. Red and green, a little blue and yellow, too. Short circuits or fuses or wires. Dynamite.

Faces in front. Square, no. Round. Eyes gleam, irises, shadows. Or pupils. Wavering edges, cheeks into lips into fangs. Teeth all pointed, gnashing. Blink. Normal, drinking beer. On a sidewalk, sitting, necks flung back. Growl at the stars. Can't see lights, just stars, a moon, only the one. She grins at me, and Devin's with her, drinking a cappuccino. Come here, come back.

Wander away. Touch a building, and the building moves. Slides away, then back again. Each brick sparking. On the ground. On gravel. Devin walks toward me.

"Where have you been?"

"Right here. Same as you."

"But I tried to find you!" Tears, real tears, drip dripping off my cheeks.

Pull them off with fingertips. Mine and Devin's tears, and they glitter. Change colour and shape. Morph into webs up our arms, collarbones, necks. Press my face to hers. Eyelashes touching. Tangling. Away, back, her face shifts. Eyebrows thicker, mouth wider. Teeth pointed, ready to strike, bite. Send venom into my bones so I can't move and get cocooned and end up an old man with no one. No one.

"Valerie, Val. It's okay."

Mallory. Not Devin. Where is she?

Mallory's nails itch for me, wriggle, elongate.

The streetlamp casts shadows, and the shadows are so many spiders clicking towards me. Legs and pincers at the ready. Bulbous bodies. They burst into falling leaves in red and gold, falling up. Gravity reversed.

Turn to the brick wall. Sparkles in the mortar. Scrape at them, try to catch them between my nails. Scratch until the brick starts to bleed. My fingers burn, and a nail rips. Bite it, chew, and swallow.

IN REVERSE

I wake with a parking lot curb for a pillow. Light the seeping stain of used tea bags in the sky. Nothing around me. Stand. Kick over six cans. The building pitches toward me, my nose. Need water, coffee, food, something. Catch my reflection in a window. Hair rumpled, greasy, pants streaked with beer and dirt. Eyes wide, too wide. Pupils engulf my irises. Blink, blink. Pale face, missing earring. The door beside my window is for a café. Organic choices advertised with kitschy designs.

A woman in front of me holds her snakeskin bag by the handle and it almost grazes the dirty, tiled floor. She steps forward and orders a cappuccino. I tell the barista I'll have the same, because I can't think too well, and part of me is convinced she is the moon. Still have my purse, wallet, debit card. Partying with rich kids means they'll leave you in a parking lot, but they won't steal your shit, so that's all right. Keep blinking, but I can feel I raise my eyebrows too high when I open my eyes. Go to the washroom. Cold water on my face, runs into my hair and down my tits. Finger comb my hair, and the strands cut open the scabs on my fingers. Unbelt the scarf and retie it over my hair so it covers my ears. Tuck in the blouse, scrub hand soap on the stains. I wish I had a toothbrush. The sink wobbles under my weight, but it's a solid block so it can't wobble. At least nothing sparks.

Back in the bustle of the café, a barista calls out a cappuccino order for Luna. The moon-lady steps forward and then we're standing beside each other because the barista made another cappuccino, this one for "Devin," and I take it in my hand. Luna looks down at me and shakes her head as if she knows I stole that name. She clatters her acrylic nails on the counter and brings her drink to her mouth. Steam floats around her afro like clouds at night.

"Darling," she says, "darling."

I wait for her to continue, but Luna breezes away and dissolves into the street. Another customer pushes into me as they reach for their coffee.

"Hey, you okay? Do you speak English?"

Blink.

The barista forces eye contact while he froths soymilk. "Do you mind taking your drink and moving out of the way so other people can pick up theirs?"

The words wash over me and I have trouble comprehending them—*darling* dancing with the other letters, curling around meaning. I blink again and it feels like my eyes crack from the pressure of my eyelids. Cement sidewalks with gaps large enough to fit a train whooshing to the back of my skull. When my eyes repair themselves, I'm sitting at the bar along the window on a metal stool. My mug full, between both hands. Drink. Hot, but not so much it burns. The foam is good, coats my teeth and tongue. Start to come back to life. I need water. I need Devin.

At the airport. Dad's gone to get breakfast, we sit with the suitcases.

"We have to come back."

"See the Eiffel and take tourist photos."

"One day. We just need one more day."

"Or maybe we could run away here. Work at a small café and learn French."

"Eat croissants and look at art."

"Get to know all the streets, and have a little apartment."

"Could you really live in a place where a cup of coffee is just an espresso shot?"

"Cappuccinos, my love." She links fingers with me. Kisses our joined hands.

There's a small mention of my hospital encounter in the newspaper. Buried in the middle pages, no picture. Safe to take the bus. They aren't the same as Calgary or Victoria. Electrical cords run from the top and through main streets. One disconnects as it rounds the corner. The driver hops out with a long pole, lifts the cord back in place and continues on, and I swear it could have been Arachne, like I've somehow found myself inside her story. Back at the beginning. A car honks, disrupts my thoughts, traffic flows.

At the bus stop a woman waits. Toe tapping.

"Hi, does this bus go to the airport?"

"No, you have to get on the Skytrain. Canada Line."

Skytrain? The station she points to looks almost like the train stations in London. But newer, shinier. A grid of tracks runs over head. I never looked up to see them before. Wait for a break in traffic so I can cross.

It looks so impressive, but from inside, it's just like the Calgary C-train, and I wish it wasn't, so I'd have something new to share with Devin. So I could tell her about this bridge in the sky, and she could tell me about the wonders she's been chasing, while we climb the Eiffel Tower together.

My cigarette pack is empty. People stand near the ashtray, and I could ask them. Smokers always help each other out. But. Devin doesn't like when I smoke. She gave up the habit when she said she did, as far as I know. No cigarette will cross the distance she left. I need to get on a plane and find her, and the ten extra minutes I take to get the ticket might mean she'll disappear again. Maybe that's been my problem—I delay and wait and justify taking my time to see her, and maybe she doesn't want to waste her time. Too busy collecting experiences to wait for me.

Besides, my throat aches, feels as if it's closing up. Constricted. Cough up mucous and spit and the vestiges of the cappuccino. A puddle, a raindrop on the pavement. Spit again and toss my lighter in the garbage can.

I wait in line at the Air Canada section. We flew Air Canada with Dad. He said it was cheapest. People have large bags on their shoulders, monstrous suitcases by their legs. Why do they need so much shit? Constant shuffle of feet and luggage. Forward half a metre. Stop. Repeat.

"Boarding pass." Attendant with a scarf tied around her throat.

"Actually, I want to buy a ticket."

"Where to?"

I run my hand over the strap of my purse. "Paris."

Click, click on her keyboard.

"We have a flight leaving at noon and one at eleven pm."

"Noon works great." My spine starts buzzing, tingling. Up and under my ribs, into my chest. I'm coming, Devin, I'm coming.

"Date of return, passport, and any bags to check?"

"Just one way. No bags." I put my passport on the counter. Take a moment to let go. The counter jumps under my thumb. Other hand to steady myself. Acid takes a while to wear off.

The attendant looks up. Frowns at my face, clothes, hair. Really sees me.

"That'll be one thousand nine hundred and sixty-four dollars, tax included." Smirks.

I open my purse and withdraw the envelope of money from my car insurance payout. I count out two grand and wait for my change. She falters. Didn't think I could pay. Thought maybe I was wasting her time. I just smile, because Devin would just smile.

Ankle jiggling over my opposite leg. Airports are all the same. People in chairs, better than waiting room chairs, but not much. A little cushioning. Conversation dull, dim. Murmurs rather than words and sentences.

A family sits near me. Dad, two daughters, three suitcases.

"Going to grab a coffee. Want one, Melanie?"

The girl with waist-length blonde hair jumps up. "Yeah, but I'll order."

The other daughter. Hoodie up, sneakers on the seat in front of her.

"You don't like coffee?"

She starts, turns just enough to see me peripherally. "No."

"Me either. My sister and dad love it."

Takes her phone out. Taps the screen.

"Last time I went to Paris, they came too. Now I'm just going to see Devin."

Hides the phone in a pocket.

We sit. Silent. Jiggle my ankle some more. I can make out the song over the speakers. An old one, Elton John. I know the words. The girl hums along. She knows, too.

"What's your name?" She asks, and I get the sense she doesn't care much, but wants some connection, some conversation that isn't with her Barbie-doll sister and her father before they go on their trip and spend all their time together.

I stare ahead. Into the space between our gate and the next.

"Levon."

She laughs. A hoot, short, but loud. Sharp and distinct.

"Like this song."

Devin stands, forearms over the rail, looking across the water, buildings, toward the Eiffel Tower. She wears a peacoat, black boots, and looks nothing like the rebel she wanted to be, but so much like herself. She turns, sees me through the tourists on the Pont des Arts. People walk in pairs or pose for pictures. I approach slowly, wait a few paces away from her.

"I was just thinking of you." Devin points to a lock on the bridge. Our initials written in permanent marker.

"You got a prosthetic after all."

We don't touch. Cautious, she pins her hair behind her ear, steps closer. I pull the sleeves of my sweater over my palms. Hunch my shoulders against the breeze off the river. I want to ask if she ever tattooed her arm, but that feels too mundane, so I don't say anything else. I rewrap my scarf around my throat.

"I knew you'd find me."

Devin reaches out first, crosses the gap between us. Fingers in my hair.

"You cut it so short."

Both my hands on her neck. I bring her face closer. Our noses touch. Devin's eyelashes blink, irises wide. This close, her features blur, and I can only see her eyes, but she shuts them. Leans into me and our lips meet.

Just for a moment, just long enough to say sorry.

When I open my eyes, she's gone, and, somehow, I'm holding the lock with our initials. I reattach it to the chain. One among tens of thousands, maybe more. But now she'll know I was here. Now she might try to find me.

Acknowledgements

Thank you to my live-in editor, biggest supporter, and first reader, Jordan Bolay. You love Elle as much as anyone, and I'm so lucky to have you cheering her (and me) on throughout this journey.

Thank you to Lissa McFarland, for providing me with the opening scene and basically every funny moment in this book (because we all know I am "very not funny" and need all the help I can get). And a huge thank you for your work creating timeline spreadsheets and copy editing the places where I started to sound "like an old person who has yet to encounter 'the internets.'"

Thank you to Aritha van Herk, for warning me about the dangers of writing picaras, and encouraging me when, heedless, I insisted on doing just that. Your ongoing support, editorial and otherwise, is unmatched and appreciated more than I can express.

Thank you to Naomi Lewis, my long-distance editor who asked all the right questions and pushed me from "why should I know that?" to completely new scenes that flesh out the story world. Your outside opinion has been crucial in strengthening this book.

Thank you to the team at UCalgary Press: Alison Cobra, Kirsten Cordingley, Melina Cusano, and Helen Hajnoczky. Your guidance and help has been invaluable as I navigated my first manuscript-length publication.

Thank you to the Flywheel reading series and the writers in Calgary for inviting me into the city's vibrant writing scene.

Thank you to the 2013/14 ENGL 598 class for your feedback on the original draft of this project; your critiques helped me find an order for many of the scenes and steered me away from awkward descriptions (like the original fence-climbing scene).

Thank you to my family and friends who have supported my writing.

As mentioned, I have taken some anecdotes and skits from Lissa McFarland to provide levity to this story. I have also referenced the names of Calgarian bands Zackariah and The Prophets, Dead Pretty, and All Hands on Jane as a tribute to those artists and the community that surrounded me during the writing of the first draft of this manuscript. I am indebted to Aritha van Herk's novel, *No Fixed Address*, as it provided the inciting incident of my writing *Disappearing in Reverse*.

Excerpts from pages six and twenty of this book originally appeared as a flash fiction piece titled "Evaporation" in *NoD Magazine*, issue number 22, published December 2017, on pages 53-54. Another excerpt from pages 188-191 of this book originally appeared as the story "Cappuccino," in *In Medias Res*, volume 23, number 1, published in winter 2018, on pages 18-20.

Photo by Jordan Bolay

ALLIE M^CFARLAND holds an MFA in Writing from the University of Saskatchewan's Department of English, where her SSHRC-funded thesis—a concise, genre-blurring, woman-centric narrative called a novel(la)—was nominated for the College of Arts & Sciences Thesis Award. Her chapbook, *Marianne's Daughters*, was published by Loft on 8th in 2018. Her poetic suite "Lullaby" (included in that chapbook) won the 2015 Dr. MacEwan Literary Arts Scholarship. She is a co-founding editor of The Anti-Languorous Project, which publishes anti*lang.* magazine, sound*bite*, Good Short Reviews, and the On Editing blog series. She is bi, drinks martinis dry, and currently runs a not-for-profit used bookstore on the unceded territories of the Lekwungen peoples of Vancouver Island where she lives with her partner and chubby cat.

BRAVE & BRILLIANT SERIES

SERIES EDITOR:
Aritha van Herk, Professor, English, University of Calgary
ISSN 2371-7238 (Print) ISSN 2371-7246 (Online)

Brave & Brilliant encompasses fiction, poetry, and everything in between and beyond. Bold and lively, each with its own strong and unique voice, Brave & Brilliant books entertain and engage readers with fresh and energetic approaches to storytelling and verse, in print or through innovative digital publication.